Also By Ashley Stoyanoff

PRG Investigations Series
Two Truths and a Lie

Deadly Trilogy
Deadly Crush
Deadly Mates
Deadly Pack

The Soul's Mark Series
The Soul's Mark: FOUND
Waking Dreams, A Soul's Mark Novella
The Soul's Mark: HUNTED
The Soul's Mark: BROKEN
The Soul's Mark: CHANGED

Dedication

For Jonel.
Thank you for being you. Your friendship is invaluable.

Chapter One

Piper

Crap, there are three of them.

Three men, dressed in jeans, dark tees, and baseball caps, standing in my driveway.

My stomach clenches and jumps. Seeing Vance again is nerve-racking enough, but all three of them ... together ...

They arrived only moments ago, parking their vehicles and getting out. They haven't made a move to approach the door yet, seemingly content to just stand there, scoping out my house. It looks as though they are talking, but the movement of their lips is so subtle that I have to squint to see it.

Swallowing thickly, I work hard to push down my jittery nerves. I should have seen this coming. Kim warned me that her cousin never works without his partners, and come to think of it, it was a rare occasion to see Vance without one or both of them, but somehow, I hadn't expected them all to show up at my house for the initial consultation.

I knew I should have gone to the grocery store. I considered it. I was going to bake cookies, and maybe some of those Pillsbury pastries.

But then, I thought about my clients and deadlines, and the reality of how far behind I am hit me. Taking time for shopping and baking ... Not really in the schedule.

And besides, Vance isn't a sweets kind of guy.

We met when Kim and I were roomies in college. He came to our apartment to install a security system the day we moved in. Then he came back to fix the bathtub faucet when it jammed and the hot water wouldn't turn off. Then there was the time that Kim's car wouldn't start and he came over to fix that, and then again, when my key got stuck and broke off in the deadbolt and we couldn't get in.

He started to come around—a lot—after the deadbolt incident, fixing things that didn't need to be fixed, and visiting with Kim. I used to see him once a week, sometimes more, and each time he came over, he stuck around for food and he always skipped dessert.

So instead of shopping and baking, knowing that the effort would be wasted on Vance, I went to the kitchen, found crackers, cheese, and some summer sausage. Not much, but enough.

Well, it would be enough as long as I took the time to arrange it to make it look like it was enough and I didn't nibble on it at all.

So that's exactly what I did. I took the time to cut the cheese and sausage, arranging it on a plate, and then I went back to my work, thinking that it would do.

Except that was when I thought only one person was coming.

Prying the blinds open further, I scan the guys over. They're all tall, well-built, and hot to boot, but it's Vance that really catches my attention.

He always catches my attention.

He isn't smiling like Jase and Wes, and he seems to be doing most of the talking. His eyes are hidden from my sight, beneath the brim of his baseball cap, but the hard set of his jaw gives me the sense that he's not impressed.

My eyes skim further down his body, taking in his broad shoulders and muscular arms. I can just make out the edges of a tattoo curling along his right bicep, peeking out from the edge of his dark tee. His hips are slim, his waist, narrow.

The man looks incredibly solid from head to toe.

He says something to the others, and they turn away from him, walking over to his truck. The tailgate is dropped, and they begin to unload boxes, stacking them in my driveway.

But Vance, he doesn't move.

His gaze sweeps the house, pausing on the living room windows, scanning them critically. Nervous energy twists a knot in my stomach. I don't have a clue what he's looking for, but the intensity of his inspection has me feeling uneasy.

After a moment, his head swivels, scanning over the left side of my house, and I get a clear view of his face. Strong cheekbones, firm jaw covered in a few days' worth of stubble, full lips, and dark eyes.

It doesn't occur to me that I'm watching him from one of the windows, until his gaze hits mine. His eyes narrow and he regards me for a moment, before a slow, cocky smile forms on his lips, melting away his hard features, giving his face a boyish quality. He lifts his chin, and then winks at me, before turning away, and moving over to the truck.

Panicked at being caught checking him out, I drop the blinds quickly, letting them fall back in place. I step back from the window, slinking further into my office, my heart thumping hard in my chest.

"My God," I whisper. He's still the hottest man I've ever seen. There's just something about him, something about all that broody swagger he has that makes me lose myself every single time I see him.

What have I gotten myself into here? I should have made Kim come for this meeting.

No. Scratch that. I shouldn't have even let her schedule it in the first place.

For a fraction of a second, I consider sitting back down at my computer, and maybe pretend that I didn't see them. If I ignore them, perhaps they'll just go away.

Okay, that's a pathetic idea.

I'm being ridiculously pathetic.

Ugh, get it together, Pipes.

It's just Vance and Jase and Wes. No big deal.

Right, okay. No big deal. I can do this.

I grab my phone, stuffing it into my back pocket, and head out of my office before I have a chance to change my mind.

I take a deep breath as I open the door, trying to calm my nerves. As I step out, closing the door behind me, Vance turns, catching my eye. He regards me peculiarly, as I start toward him.

Trying to ignore the way my heart is racing in my chest, each beat pounding through my body painfully fast, I force a bright smile and lift my hand, offering a little wave. "Hey, Vance."

Oh God, did I just wave? I swallow down a groan as a hot flush spreads through my cheeks. Crap, I did, didn't I?

Way to play it cool, Pipes.

The corners of his lips twitch, revealing a slight smile, and he chuckles.

My God that sound … it's hard and rough and beautiful.

My heart smiles, and my stomach flutters for a moment, but I quickly push it away. I'm really not the stomach fluttering type, or at least I try not to be.

"Hey, Piper," he says, striding toward me. "Sorry we're late."

I glance at my watch, my brow drawing in, confused. Our meeting was scheduled for one, and it's only a few minutes past. Not what I'd call late.

Shaking my head, I meet his eyes once more as he stops in front of me, letting out a nervous laugh. "Not a problem," I say. "You're not late at all."

He says nothing, regarding me for a moment, his eyes tracing my face intently. I can't tell what he's thinking, though that's not really a surprise. I could never get a read on him before either.

Swallowing thickly, I force my eyes away from him and glance at the growing pile of boxes, waving a hand toward it. "What's all that?"

He eyes me curiously for a moment, smirking. "It's your new security system."

My brow furrows in confusion, and I turn back to him, catching his eye. "Pardon?"

"It's your new security system," he repeats, a flash of

amusement passing across his face. "Picked it up this morning."

Um … what?

What the heck?

I blink, certain I'm looking at him as though he's insane. "You, uh, already bought a security system? Without even knowing what I'm looking for?"

"What else was I supposed to do?" he asks, arching an eyebrow in question. "Let you go without so you can consider your options while you've got a goddamn stalker lurking?"

I roll my eyes. "I don't have a stalker."

"I picked it up," he continues, ignoring my response, "because I couldn't in good conscience leave you here without it."

I stare at him incredulously, not sure what to say. I don't know if I should be annoyed that he took such a liberty, or touched that he wants to make sure I'm safe.

I'm still contemplating how to respond when I hear footsteps, and I glance over to see Jase and Wes sauntering toward us, arms loaded with boxes.

"Hey, guys," I say, waving again. "Good to see you again."

Jase grins, flashing a dimple. "Hey, Piper."

"Yo," Wes says, lifting his chin. "You mind if we take this stuff inside?"

Feeling slightly uneasy, I glance at the boxes, noting that there are still quite a few sitting in the driveway. "Um, I'm not sure I need all of that."

"It's already paid for, Piper," Vance says. "No returns."

"Right," I mutter, rolling my eyes and giving him a look. "Of course it is."

Vance chuckles at my look, amusement touching his eyes, as he gives me a look of his own, cocking a brow, almost daring me to argue with him.

Flustered, I scramble backward to the door and push it open. I nearly trip over my own feet, but catch myself before I tumble, offering them a frazzled smile. "Come on in."

Vance steps inside, Jase and Wes following him. I close the door behind them as I watch them scope out my place, their eyes scanning everything, cataloging, assessing. My first instinct is to ask them what they're looking for, but I hold the question back, instead asking, "Um … Can I get you something to drink? I have beer, rye, coolers, or I can make some …"

I'm about to ramble off that it will only take a couple minutes to make some coffee when Vance says, "A glass of water would be great."

Nodding, I walk quickly toward the kitchen. I'm overly aware of them moving around my house, checking locks, bringing in more boxes, as I retrieve three glasses from the cupboard and fill them with water from the Brita. Once filled, I wedge a tumbler in between my right arm and torso, grabbing the second and third with my hands. I don't bother grabbing the cheese, sausage and crackers, because I know it's not going to cut it. There's barely enough for two, let alone four.

They are talking in low voices when I come out of the kitchen, standing in the living room. Juggling the drinks, I maneuver around the boxes stacked through the room, careful not to spill, and hand them out.

Vance's eyes follow me the entire time.

My stomach flutters once more as I hand Vance his water, though this time, it's not a pleasant feeling. There's an odd expression on his face that takes me a moment to place. *Annoyance.*

"The place looks good," he grumbles after a beat. "No goddamn security, but it's *nice.*"

Nice. My eyes narrow and my shoulders straighten. What a crappy word. It's an open concept bungalow with floor to ceiling windows and French doors overlooking the backyard. Fourteen-foot ceilings, and stainless steel appliances. Everything is modern, and decorated perfectly.

My place isn't *nice,* it's incredible.

Before I can tell him exactly what I think of his assessment, Wes says, "Gonna need to replace the lock on the French doors. Wouldn't take much to pick it, or snap it with the right tools."

"The door from the garage into the house needs a new lock, too," Jase adds, turning to look at me, his lips drawn tight.

"There's locks on the windows," I say with slight offence, even though I know they are right. The security here sucks. "And a deadbolt and chain lock on the door."

"Jesus, Piper," Vance grinds out, glaring at me. "Kim said you needed an update, not a full-blown overhaul. You've been here six months now. You should have called. I would have put in a goddamn system when you moved in."

I open my mouth, and then close it when nothing comes out. They've only just gotten their drinks, and they already look as though they want to throttle me.

Crapsicles. This isn't going well.

Vance

Piper folds her arms over her breasts, shifting from foot to foot. She blinks at me, and her mouth keeps opening and closing, as though she wants to say something, but she can't find the right words.

It's been almost six months since I've seen her last and I swear the woman is more beautiful now than she ever was. I scan her instinctively, exhaling slowly, keeping my expression blank. Her skin is smooth, the color of cream, and her nose and cheeks are dotted with freckles. Her long, naturally red hair is pulled back into a braid that hangs down her back. She's wearing a black ribbed tank top and the skinniest jeans I've ever seen, making her look curvy as hell, and with the way her arms are folded over her breasts, I can see the edges of her bra at her sides. I can't stop myself from wondering if her underwear is made of the same hot pink lace.

The thought momentarily distracts me.

Her eyes dart around the room, looking anywhere but at me. She's always been a little shy around me, and has never been very talkative, but she looks even more anxious than normal, which I guess makes sense since I'm clearly angry, but it's only because she's being careless.

I should have come over here when she first moved in. I

thought about it. I almost offered, too. But she's always so goddamn nervous around me that I figured she'd just blow me off.

She always blows me off.

Always has an excuse.

But Christ, I thought she had more sense than this. If I wanted to get into this house, I figure I could do it in about two minutes flat.

And that would be taking my time.

Silence ensues as I wait for some kind of response from her. For the first time in probably forever, Wes and Jase keep their mouths shut, seemingly content to just watch us. I'm pretty sure they're just as pissed off as I am, seeing the crap locks on her house, and the lack of any kind of security. She didn't even put in window alarms, and you can find those at the goddamn dollar store.

Seconds tick by. Five, maybe ten, before Piper looks at me. She unconsciously hugs her arms tighter over her breasts, pushing them together and making her cleavage pop further. "Um ... I don't really know you, Vance," she says, scrunching her freckle dotted nose. "I'm not entirely sure why you'd think I'd call you to put in a security system."

I snort, arching a brow. What a bullshit excuse. She might have avoided me. She might have even gone as far to run the other way every time she saw me coming, but she knows me. "You've got my number on your phone listed as badass hottie and it's been there since that first day you moved in with Kim. I'm gonna guess that you haven't deleted it."

Timidly, Piper ducks her head, refusing to meet my eyes as pink creeps up her neck, settling into her cheeks.

It's a gorgeous shade.

"Oh my God," she mumbles under her breath. "I'm going to kill Kim."

Wes laughs, but it comes out as a wheezing choking sound, as though he's trying to swallow it. He turns his back to us, walking over to the French doors and bending down as though he is inspecting the lock further. He's not. I'm certain he's just trying to hide the shit-eating grin splitting his face.

"You should have used the number," I say. "You shouldn't have fuckin' waited this long."

"Vance … I, uh …" She presses her lips together and her jaw ticks as though she's grinding her teeth. "I don't really know what to tell you. I didn't think I needed it."

"Obviously, you were wrong," I say. "You wouldn't have called Kim to get in touch with me otherwise." I know I'm being a dick, but I can't help it. You'd think after everything I did to make sure her and Kim's apartment was safe, she'd take at least a few simple precautions.

"You about done, Vance?" Jase asks, annoyance thick in his voice. Whether it's at me or at the situation I'm not entirely sure, but he's glaring at me; I can feel it, though I can't pull my eyes away from Piper to glare back at him.

I almost tell him to fuck off, but I bite it back. "Yeah, I'm done."

From my peripheral vision, I notice him move toward the couch and take a seat. He sets his glass down on the coffee table, and then leans forward, resting his forearms on his knees and dangling his hands between them.

"Why don't you tell us what's been going on, Piper," he says, managing a gentle and encouraging tone.

She frowns, unfolding her arms and looking around, avoiding my face. "Didn't Kim already explain all this to you guys?"

He nods. "She said you have a stalker, but I wanna hear what's been going on from you."

"I don't have a stalker," she says tersely, her jaw tightening. "Someone's been messing with me, but it's not a stalker."

"Gonna need a little more than that, babe," Wes says, as he crosses the room and takes a seat next to Jase. He leans back, extending one arm along the back of the couch, crossing his right leg over his left knee, and rests his glass on his thigh. "What do you mean someone's been messing with you?"

She hesitates, her eyes flickering to me again. I can see her concern as she fidgets with her clothing. "Um, well," she says, her voice quiet, passive. "Ten days ago, someone threw a brick through my front window. Nine days ago, someone keyed my truck right in my driveway. Eight days ago, someone spray painted the words 'stay away' across my garage door." She laughs once, shaking her head. "That one really pissed me off. The jerk didn't even have the courtesy to tell me what the hell I need to stay away from." She stalls for a tick, her jaw tightening once more. "Each day it's something new, a new piece of my property vandalized."

"So you want us to find who's doing this?" I say.

Piper looks at me, her expression turning hard. "No, I don't want you to find anyone. All I want is a security system. Something with cameras so the police can ID the person."

I move in front of her, meeting her gaze straight on. My eyes narrow, as I stare at her for a moment. It's peculiar to me how casually she talks about her situation, as though having someone threaten her and destroy her property is no big deal, but there's something about her voice that sounds off, and I catch the uneasy look on her face. "What's really going on here, Piper?"

She looks away from me, her gaze shifting over my shoulder, and she shrugs helplessly. "If I knew that," she says, "I wouldn't want video surveillance, would I?"

Chapter Two

Piper

I'm sitting in my home office, staring at my computer. I should be working. I have four deadlines coming up next week and I've barely begun the projects. I'm a book cover designer and I have clients counting on me, but I just can't focus. I'm too exhausted to really get anything done, too distracted to concentrate.

And it really doesn't help that I can hear the guys moving around the house, hammering and drilling, doors opening and closing.

Leaning back in my leather office chair, I prop my feet up on my desk and cross my legs at the ankles. My muscles are strained, coiled along my shoulders, stretched through my neck and back. My mind is stuck on all the stuff Vance is installing in my house. Door sensors, window sensors, motion detectors, video surveillance … The alarm system they are installing is completely over-the-top and definitely not what I would have chosen, but I've got to admit I'm oddly nervous and excited that Vance has gone to so much trouble for me.

My cell phone chirps and I lean forward, picking it up from my desk to take a look. It's a text message from Kim.

Kim: How did it go?

I sit there for a moment, clutching my phone, staring at the message, before I start laughing. I just laugh, shaking my head. I bet she knows exactly how it went.

I consider how to respond, debating on whether I should give her hell now, or wait until I see her, before I take hold of my phone with both hands, punching in my response.

> Me: I think I might hate you.

> Kim: LOL. Meeting went well, I take it.

> Me: You have no idea. Oh, wait. That's right, you do have an idea. I can't believe you told him!

> Kim: You need more than some stupid security system. I told him for your own good.

> Me: Seriously? How is him knowing that he's in my phone under badass hottie for my own good?

> Kim: Oh shit. Oh shit. Oh shit. He told you? He wasn't supposed to tell you.

I imagine her cringing and smirk. Good, I hope she feels bad. Serves her right.

> Me: Well, he did, and he did it in front of Jase and Wes. He also brought a ridiculously high tech alarm system with him. They are installing it now.

> Kim: I figured he would.

> Me: You should have warned me.

Kim: You would have cancelled.

I tilt my head as I read the text, thinking that she's probably right. I would have canceled. The truth is, I didn't want to use Vance in the first place.

The man makes me nervous.

Beyond nervous.

He always has.

There's just something there, something special about him that pulls me in, yet, twists me up.

But Kim insisted, telling me he would flip if he found out I hired someone else and that knowing him, he'd probably end up ripping it out and installing a new one.

I let out a deep sigh, as I type out another message.

Me: You also told him I have a stalker.

Kim: It's for your own good, Pipes.

I roll my eyes.

Me: I don't have a stalker.

Kim: Whatever. Just let them do their thing. It's what they do.

Stifling a groan, I almost point out that all they are doing is installing an alarm system, but I don't. I'm just too tired to deal with it right now.

Me: We still on for tomorrow night?

Kim: Hell, yeah. I need a girl's night.

Me: K, gotta get back to work. Later.

Kim: Later.

Sighing, and swinging my legs off my desk, I put my phone aside and turn back to the computer, trying to get some work done.

Vance

"Yo, Vance," Wes calls as he comes into the kitchen. "You seen Piper?"

"She's working," I say, reaching up over the sink, and placing a sensor on the window frame. "What do you need?"

He stares at me for a tick. "I'm ready to start on the monitors. You know where she wants them?"

I consider the placement for a moment, even consider going and asking her, but I don't. I'm still too pissed off that she didn't call me sooner, and knowing her, she'll probably just tell me she doesn't want them installed anywhere.

Grabbing the receiver, I line it up with the sensor, before affixing it to the windowsill. "Office, bedroom, and living room."

He nods and begins to turn away, but hesitates, looking back at me. "You planning on leaving this at just a system install?"

Pausing, I turn back to him. I don't respond immediately, because I honestly don't know what to say. Piper made it clear she doesn't want me involved, but the thought of leaving this alone makes a knot twist in my gut. "And if I'm not?"

He grins, shrugging one shoulder. "Then I'd ask you what you know about her."

Stopping what I'm doing, I put the receiver down and turn to him, leaning against the counter and folding my arms over my chest.

What do I know about her?

A hell of a lot.

I know she's twenty-three. She's from Indiana, came to

Sacramento for school, and finished her degree in graphic design six months early. She has a sister who is twenty-one and a brother who is eighteen. Her parents died when she was eleven, and her grandmother raised her. She has two credit cards, which she religiously pays off every month, two days before the bill comes in. She owns her house, no mortgage, paid for it with her trust fund, and she's self-employed, her business, designing book covers.

I know other things, too. Like she loves chocolate. She prefers beer or rye over any fruity drink, and she has a bottle opener on her keychain. She uses coconut moisturizer. She loves shoes, but not as much as handbags. She enjoys music— anything from country to rock to hip-hop, she thinks pick-up trucks are sexy, and she looks fucking incredible in jeans and a pair of cowboy boots.

Yeah, I know lots of things about Piper Clare Owen.

But instead of telling him all of that, I say, "She's Kim's friend."

Wes snorts, cutting me a disbelieving look. "You telling me you didn't run a background check on her when she moved in with Kim?"

I damn near flinch when he says it, the shock and subtle anger in his voice making me feel like an ass. But what am I supposed to say? That I know lots about her, but none of it will help with an investigation? Am I supposed to tell him her favorite drinks, or what moisturizer she uses?

Shaking my head, I turn back to the window. I'm too annoyed, too frustrated to be having this conversation right now. I've spent the last two hours installing window sensors and motion detectors, and I just want to finish it and get out of here.

I need to clear my head.

I need to figure out what to do next.

Wes doesn't seem to pick up on my frustration and he keeps talking. "It's fine. I'll run a check. See if I can find anything."

This time I do flinch, and I turn back to him, my response, immediate. "No, you won't."

Wes says nothing, but I can tell by the way his face twitches that he's biting down on his cheek, trying not to laugh.

I glare at him.

The bastard already knows.

He knows I've already done the background check.

He knows I just don't want to share.

He knows and he's just trying to get under my goddamn skin.

Before I have a chance to tell him to fuck off, Jase strolls into the kitchen, smiling wide. "He won't what?"

Wes laughs, glancing at him. "Vance doesn't want me looking into Piper."

Jase looks from Wes, to me, his brow dipping with a frown. "You saying we're not going to look into this for her?"

"I didn't say that," I grumble. "I said I don't want Wes running background checks."

Jase doesn't respond right away, contemplating my words. Folding his arms over his chest and leaning a hip against the counter, he regards me curiously for a few seconds, but eventually he chuckles and shakes his head. "Good," he says, "because I already called Cruz. They've got nothing, no leads, and no suspects."

"What about the ex?" Wes asks. "What was his name? Craig? Cameron? Chuck? It was something with a C. Didn't they date all through college?"

"Colton," I say, without thought. "They dated for two and a half years and they broke it off when they graduated. He took a job out of state. It was a mutual break-up. No hard feelings."

Jase and Wes stare at me.

And stare at me.

And stare at me some more.

It's Wes who cracks a grin first, raising a questioning eyebrow. "Thought all you knew about her is that she's Kim's friend."

I turn my eyes toward him and glare, as the corners of his lips twitch spasmodically. He's usually better at keeping a straight face, but today he can't seem to hide his amusement.

I grit my teeth. Glad he's finding this so funny.

A cell phone ringing distracts me from the moment. It's Jase's. Digging it out of his pocket, he glances at the screen and grins as he answers it. "Hey, darlin'." He pauses for a beat, his smile fading. "What do you mean you bought a truck? You're not driving back."

Wes groans, cutting me a look. "Shit."

I nod. That pretty much sums it up.

It's been nearly three weeks since Jase came home without Elena, leaving her in New York. After spending a year on the run, hiding from her abusive cop fiancée, she needed space, needed time with her parents.

But he's been a goddamn mess worrying about her.

Worrying that she won't come home.

Worrying that she might hate him for killing Lawrence Peck, even though the bastard shot Jase's dad, and pointed a gun at both of them.

Now he's going to be freaking out about her driving all the way back to Sacramento alone.

"No, you are not," Jase says, his voice a near growl. He pushes off from the counter, paces a few steps, and his jaw begins to tick. "Jesus, Elena, I don't care what color the truck is. I don't want you driving. It's too far."

I shake my head and swallow down my laughter, exchanging a look with Wes. Did she really just try to use the truck's color to talk him into this?

"I'll pay to ship your stuff here," Jase continues. "Hell, I'll buy you new stuff. You're not fuckin' driving."

Jase pauses for a beat, and then he pulls his phone away from his ear, glancing at the screen, his frown deepening. "She hung up on me," he mutters, shaking his head. "I can't believe she hung up on me."

Wes full out laughs. "Good for her. I'd hang up on you, too."

Rolling his eyes, Jase flips Wes off, before he groans, raking a hand down his face. "Shit," he mutters, the grip on his phone tightening. "Shit, shit, shit."

"Don't worry about it, buddy," I say. "She's probably

stressing out just as much as you are. Give her a few minutes and call her back, yeah?"

"Yeah," he mumbles, turning away. "I'm gonna go pick up the new locks. You guys need anything else?"

"Secondary deadbolt for the front door," I say. "Thicker chain lock, too."

Jase shakes his head, glancing back at me. "She doesn't need ..."

"I want it, Jase," I say, cutting him off. "I don't want to have to worry about her here."

"If you're worried," Wes says, "you can always do what Jase did."

Looking at him, Jase cocks an eyebrow. "What's that?"

Wes shrugs. "Move in with her."

Jase says nothing to that, but he does laugh as he turns away, heading for the door, and I shake my head, smile, and then, before turning back to my work, I say to Wes, "Don't you have a monitor to install?"

Piper

The day slips by painstakingly slow, minutes feeling like hours, hours feeling like days, but I do manage to get some work done. I finish a cover draft and email it off for the author's approval, I spend some time scanning through photo stock, trying to find the perfect images, but mostly, I just stare at my computer blankly, waiting for the guys to finish up and leave.

I've come to the realization that I'm not going to get much more done today. I considered going out there a few times to see how the installation is coming along. It's not like I'm actually getting anything done in here, but I'm not ready to face Vance just yet, not after the whole *badass hottie* thing, especially when I'm pretty sure he's still pissed off at me.

I click on another photo, enlarging it and studying it, when the sound of footsteps coming down the hallway draws my attention. I hold my breath as they grow near, hoping that whoever it is will keep going, but they don't, pausing outside my office door, and then someone knocks.

Sighing, I push back my chair and stand up, walking over to the door, opening it slowly. Vance stands in the hallway with two boxes, one small and one large, in hand.

"What's up?" I ask, and then clear my throat. I'm so nervous. He's smiling, a glimmer of amusement touching his dark eyes, but there's also something … agitated in his gaze. Is he still mad? Does it matter if he is? I've spent the last few hours convincing myself that I don't care if he's mad at me, but the thing is, I totally care.

"We're almost done," he says, as his gaze slides past me, surveying my office. "Just need to install a sensor on the window in here and set up the last monitor. Mind if I come in?"

Slowly, I nod when he meets my eyes again. "Um … yeah, sure," I mumble. "Come on in."

He walks into the room, smirking at me cockily as he makes a point of shutting the door behind him.

I feel my face flush as he makes his way over to my filing cabinet. He shifts a stack of papers aside and sets down the boxes, before pulling out a pocket knife and slicing them open.

Hesitating for a moment, feeling slightly uncomfortable, I move over to my desk and sit back down.

This doesn't have to be awkward, I tell myself. *So what if he knows I think he's hot. It'll only be awkward if I let it be.*

Vance rifles through the boxes, pulling out a sensor, and steps over to the window. He fiddles with the pieces, pulling them apart, and then with a measuring tape and pencil, he begins marking the windowsill.

Silence swallows the room for a few seconds, before he asks, "How's business been?"

"Good," I say, keeping my eyes on the computer screen, clicking through images once more. "Busy."

"You still doing websites?" he asks, glancing over at me quickly, before returning his focus to the window.

"Some," I respond.

"Not sure if Kim told you, but we're opening an office," he

tells me. "You should chat with Jase's woman, Elena, when she gets back in town. She's gonna be running the place and we're gonna need a site built. Maybe you can do it."

No, Kim didn't tell me. The last I heard, the PRG Investigations team only works on a referrals basis and it keeps them busy. Crazy busy. Why would they want to open an office?

I open my mouth, planning to ask a bunch of questions, but all that comes out is, "Sure."

Vance chuckles beside me. His eyes scan me for a second, a look of curiosity on his face. "We're back to one word conversations, I see."

I cut my eyes to him, feeling my cheeks heat with another flush, hotter than before, and mumble, "Sorry."

He chuckles again. "It's okay, honey. I'll take whatever I can get."

I let out a nervous laugh. What does he mean by that? I'm not sure what to say, or how I should feel, or even what to think, so I say nothing, do nothing. I just stare back at him.

Ugh, this is so awkward.

He stands there for a long moment, watching me, before the corner of his lip twitches up with a small smirk, and then he shakes his head, turning back to the window.

I turn back around and start looking through photos again, determined to find what I need.

It takes him a little over twenty minutes to install the sensor and new monitor. I feel his eyes touch me every few minutes, although he doesn't say a word.

It's not exactly uncomfortable, though not entirely comfortable either.

It's not the first time I've felt him observing me. I felt it the day I moved out of Kim's place, too. He'd been there, watching me pack. He never said a word to me then, either, but I felt his eyes following me around the house.

I try to ignore it. I really, really try, but I can't, and when he finally finishes setting everything up, I nearly sigh in relief.

But then he calls me over to show me how the system works and I realize he's not done.

Eight cameras, three different kinds of alarms. At home settings, away settings. He shows me how to pull up the cameras, tests all the different alarms so I know what they sound like. He tells me where all the monitors are, and then he helps me program a code.

It takes another forty-five minutes to go through everything I need to know about the system, and by the time he's finished, I'm ready to tell him to take it all out. It's just too much.

But I don't.

Of course I don't.

Instead, I write him a check for the alarm system, and then walk with him to the door, noticing for the first time that Jase and Wes are already gone.

When we reach the door, Vance opens it, and then he turns back to me. He stands there for a moment, staring down at me as though there's something on his mind, but he's not sure if he should say it.

Not wanting this to get awkward again, I smile softly. "It was really good to see you again, Vance. Thank you so much for doing all this. I really appreciate it."

"Piper," he says, and then sighs. "I'm gonna ask around, see what I can find out about the shit that's been going on here."

I shake my head. "No. I don't want you to do that, Vance."

He frowns, narrowing his eyes at me as he crosses his arms over his chest, making his already large biceps bulge, as he regards me with what looks like frustration mixed with anger.

"The police are on it," I blurt, suddenly feeling the need to explain why I don't want him poking around. "With the cameras installed, I'm sure they'll catch the person quickly."

He stares at me for a moment, looking as though he's about to argue, but then his expression shifts, and the corner of his mouth turns up in a half smile, before it spreads into a full-blown grin. "You've got my number. Use it. Anytime."

"I, uh ... I will," I stammer as butterflies swarm my belly. He wants me to call him? Oh God, he wants me to call him. *Anytime.*

"I'm serious, Piper," he says, his voice firm but still, soft, warm. "Use it."

"I will," I assure him, and I will, maybe—sometime.

He nods, seemingly content, and he takes a few steps, backing out the door. "Later, Piper."

"Later," I say.

When the door shuts behind him, I try not to smile, but fail. Miserably.

Chapter Three

Vance

My cell phone beeps and I open my eyes.

I'm on my back on the couch in my living room, one foot on the floor, the other hanging over the armrest. The lights are still on, so is the television, some infomercial playing, and I'm still fully dressed.

"Shit," I mutter, sitting up and rubbing at the kink in my neck. My muscles ache, my back is stiff. I've gotta stop falling asleep like this. I've got a bed. A comfortable bed. When was the last time I slept in it?

Last week?

The week before that?

A month ago?

Shit, I don't even know.

My cell phone beeps again and I groan, reaching for it and checking the display, and I feel my eyebrows knit together at what I see there. *Piper's house. Rear door motion detected.*

Suddenly fully alert, I tap the screen, unlocking the phone and accessing the security system app. My foot beats restlessly against the hardwood floor as I wait for the video feed to load, watching the words *acquiring signal* flash on the screen.

It feels like hours, although it's probably only seconds, before the image finally begins to load, pixel by goddamn pixel.

I narrow my eyes, scanning the small image on my screen. The motion lights above the French doors have been triggered, lighting up her back patio and standing there, hand on the door handle, face pressed up to the glass, peeking in, is a man. I can't see his face, or anything identifying for that matter. He's covered head-to-toe in dark clothing, with what looks like a wallet chain dangling from his jeans, and a hood pulled up over his head.

"Shit," I mutter again, shooting up from the couch. Fire hits my gut, and it makes no sense. I knew at some point someone would be sneaking around her place and I'd get the alarm, but goddamnit, if actually seeing the bastard there doesn't piss me off.

Scooping up my keys and wallet off the coffee table, I head for the door, grabbing my shoes off the floor and yanking them on, and then I bolt out of my apartment.

Not waiting for the elevator, I head for the stairs, jogging down the six flights with my cell phone in hand. As I move through the stairwell, I thumb through my phone for Wes's number, tap on it, and bring the phone to my ear.

He answers on the second ring. "Yo."

"A motion alarm is going off at Piper's," I say. "There's a guy standing at her French doors. Looks like he's trying to get in."

"You've got to be shitting me," he says, his voice dry with sleep. "I thought this was just a vandal."

"Me, too," I say as I hit the lobby. I cross it with a few long strides and push my way through the doors. "I'm heading there now. You busy?"

"On my way," he says, sounding more awake. "You want me to call Jase?"

I hesitate for a tick, before responding. "No. Let him sleep. He needs it."

"Got it," Wes mumbles as the sound of fabric rustling hits my ear. "See you in a few."

"Later," I say and then thumb the screen, ending the call.

Outside my apartment, I jog over to my truck, and haul my

ass up into it, starting it up, and then I take off in the direction of Piper's house.

A few minutes later, my phone beeps again, the display now reading: *Piper's house. Front door motion detected.*

Piper

A stream of subtle beeps fill my ears, and disoriented, I open my eyes.

I'm on my stomach in my bed surrounded by pillows, one tucked on each side with my arms curled around them, holding them close, two under my head, and one under my belly. The lights are off, the room, dark, aside from an annoying red light that keeps flashing from somewhere.

Half asleep and out of it, I roll over and push the pillows aside, sitting up. A glance at the clock tells me it's nearly five o'clock in the morning, and I scrub at my face, blinking rapidly, trying to clear the sleepy haze clouding my head.

The beeping persists, growing steadily louder. It takes a few moments for the source of the sound to sink in, but when it does, I'm suddenly wide awake.

Oh shit. It's the motion detector, not a full alarm, but a somewhat subtle warning that someone is close to a door or window.

Slowly, I shift my eyes to the screen and I swallow thickly, reading the warning flashing there. *Rear door motion detected.*

Oh shit.

Rear door motion detected.

Oh shit.

Oh shit.

Oh shit.

Someone's here. Someone's at my back door.

My panic surfaces quickly, and instinctively, I grab a pillow, hugging it to my torso. I can feel my anxiety rising, closing up my throat. My heart pounds, thumping in my chest painfully quick.

Okay ... *Don't panic*, I tell myself. *You can handle this. Just get up, and pull up the camera. It's probably just a raccoon, or a stray cat. There's nothing to worry about.*

Right, okay. Nothing to worry about.

I let go of the pillow and get out of bed. My nerves are a frazzled mess as I cross the room, silently pleading to the monitor to let this be a false alarm.

Carefully, I touch the screen just like Vance showed me, pulling up the video feed for the rear door, and what I see there makes my panic resurface, rising up my throat like bile. There's a man, or at least I think it's a man. Tall, lanky, and dressed in black, with a hood pulled up over his head, hiding his features. His hand is on the doorknob, rattling the French doors.

After a moment, he lets go. He doesn't retreat right away, standing there staring at the door, before shoving his hands in his pockets, and stepping out of sight of the camera.

But the beeping doesn't stop and moments later, the monitor flashes again, this time reading: *front door motion detected*, and I quickly pull up the front door video feed only to find the man now standing at my front door. He shakes the doorknob, before throwing his hands up in the air.

My heart stalls, rendering me motionless, before it starts pounding so hard it hurts my chest. This alarm system was supposed to make me feel safer, but oh my God, seeing someone outside, trying to get in ... I think I prefer not knowing.

I need to do something.

I need to call the police.

I start to turn away, going for my phone, when the man on the screen shifts, looking up, and I catch a glimpse of the face.

My brow furrows and it takes a few seconds for recognition to settle in, but when it does, I sag in relief, nearly collapsing onto the floor.

It's Jimmy.

I blink at the screen. What the hell is he doing here at five o'clock in the morning?

No. Scratch that. What the hell is he doing here at all? He

should still be in Denver, working a photo shoot.

My heart is still pounding, my stomach, still in knots, as I make my way through the house, toward the front door, flipping on lights as I go. It takes me a moment to disarm the alarm, having to enter the code three times before I get it right.

"Hey, Pipes," Jimmy says as I pull open the door, grinning. "Something's wrong with my key."

He steps past me, strolling into the house, kicking off his shoes as he goes. I watch him incredulously as he moves straight for the kitchen, pulling the fridge open and sticking his head in. I want to be mad. He just scared the daylights out of me. But I can't drudge up the emotion, when all I feel is relief that it's him and not someone actually trying to break into my house.

Rolling my eyes, I lock the door and reset the alarm, before I follow him, asking, "What are you doing here, Jimmy?"

He pulls his head out of the fridge, raising his eyebrows. "I sent you an email."

I shake my head. "You didn't send an email."

"Well, I meant to," he says, giving me a bashful look as he pulls out a carton of eggs and milk from the fridge, setting them on the counter, and then moves over to the bread box, opening it and retrieving a loaf. "Why did you change the locks on me?"

I'm about to tell him that I didn't change the locks on him exactly—maybe even remind him that he doesn't actually live here, and he was supposed to give me back my keys when Kim and I returned from Mexico last month—when I'm distracted by the sound of a vehicle pulling into my driveway.

Vance

Every light in Piper's house is on when I pull into the driveway, and fire hits my gut once more as I imagine her inside, nervously studying the monitors, looking for the asshole that's been messing with her.

Turning off my truck, I don't wait for Wes, snagging my phone off the seat and folding out. I shut the door quietly, before striding toward the house, careful as I scan the property in the shadows of predawn, noticing that everything looks untouched. Whoever it was must have bolted when she turned on the lights.

As I approach the front door, my phone begins to buzz again, this time the motion sensors picking me up, and with the quick twist of the knob, I find the door locked.

I hesitate for a moment, slowly lowering my hand from the doorknob. I fiddle with my keys, fingering the one for her house, before sticking it in the lock and letting myself in. I only make it a step into the house when I hear a man's laughter coming from the kitchen.

She has a goddamn man over.

My jaw ticks and my hands twitch as a mix of irritation and something that I don't particularly want to give a name to, washes over me. It feels slimy and slippery and I don't like it one bit. I'm possessive over my family, that much is true, but Piper isn't family so I can't justify why the guy in the kitchen makes me want to throw him down and break each bone in his face one by one.

I feel myself growing hot, and I take a deep breath, trying to keep my anger down.

I don't have a right to be mad.

I should be relieved that she wasn't alone when the alarm went off.

But I'm not.

The steady beeping of the alarm begins, signaling that the door is open, and I close it, before moving to the panel and punching in the code quickly, quieting the alarm.

"Vance," Piper says from behind me. "What are you doing here?"

I turn to her, my jaw tightening when I see how she's dressed. Tiny little black shorts, showing off lots of leg, and a tight light blue tank showing off too much cleavage.

My gut reaction is to tell her to put some damn clothes on, but I manage to swallow the words down.

"Morning, Piper," I say calmly, keeping my voice steady as to not betray my irritation.

She regards me for a beat, her brow wrinkling in confusion. "How did you get in?"

I smirk at her, stepping away from the alarm panel, jingling my keys in my hand. "I used my key."

She stares at me, the panic in her eyes dissolving into confusion. She doesn't respond right away, her gaze shifting from my face, her brow furrowing as her eyes fall to my key ring dangling from my finger.

"Your key," she says slowly, her eyes coming back to mine, quickly flaring with annoyance. "When exactly did I give you a key?"

Slowly, I stroll over to her, pausing right in front of her, so close, her breasts graze against my chest. I don't answer her question because her tone tells me that any answer I give will definitely be the wrong one, so instead, I bring my lips to her ears, keeping my voice low as I ask my own question. "Who's the guy in the kitchen?"

Piper tenses, her body suddenly so rigid that it trembles slightly as a shiver passes through her. It surprises me that she doesn't step away, instead, her body seems to tilt into mine, leaning closer.

I don't know what to make of it.

She smells so goddamn good, like sunshine and sweetness.

My hands itch to wrap around her waist, my arms wanting to pull her closer, make sure she's okay, but I force myself not to.

When she doesn't answer, I ask again. "Who is he, Piper?"

"Jimmy," she says softly. "He's a photographer I use regularly."

"Jimmy," I repeat, confused. "A photographer."

Piper nods. "Yes."

I take a step back from her, needing to put some distance in between us before I end up wrapping her in my arms. "What's he doing here?"

Piper narrows her eyes, watching as I fold my arms over my chest, and she places a hand on her hip. "What are you doing here?"

"Your motion sensor alarm went off," I grind out, irritated. "So I came over."

Piper just stares at me.

And stares.

And stares.

She's waiting for an explanation. I can see it in her eyes, but I don't know what else to tell her.

Her alarm went off and I came over.

It's as simple as that.

When I say nothing else, she lets out a sigh, and realizing that I'm not going to elaborate, she casts a disbelieving look my way. "Please tell me you're not watching my house, Vance."

I stare at her and she tilts her head to the side, staring right back at me. She doesn't look entirely put off by the thought of me watching her house, but she also doesn't seem happy about it either.

I decide not to answer.

"You didn't call," I say.

"Um … no, I didn't," she agrees.

"I told you to call me anytime," I continue. "Your alarm going off, with all the shit that's been happening, seems like a pretty good time to use that number, don't you think?"

"Well, yeah," she says, "but it was a false alarm."

"A false alarm," I repeat, narrowing my eyes. "Piper, I saw the guy trying to get into your house."

"Piper?" Jimmy the photographer calls as he steps into the doorway of the kitchen, hesitating as he glances between us. "Do you guys want breakfast?"

My eyes slice to him and I stare, taking him in. He's in black jeans with a wallet chain dangling at his side, a black hoodie, has dark brown hair with frosted tips, a lip ring, and an eyebrow ring. He's tall, maybe only an inch shorter than my six-foot-two frame, but he's skinny.

He's the guy I saw on the monitor.

"Um, yeah, but uh …" Piper starts, but stalls, glancing at me. "But Vance won't be staying. He's got a … um … meeting to get to."

I glance at Piper, cocking an eyebrow. "I've got a meeting?"

Piper says nothing, but she slowly nods, refusing to meet my eyes. She fidgets with the strap of her tank, and then tugs on the bottom of her shorts, as though attempting to make the skintight fabric look longer, before moving on with an attempt to tame her bedhead.

She's nervous.

I stand there watching her fix her appearance, feeling oddly satisfied that it's my presence that's making her nervously fidget and not *Jimmy the photographer's*.

Silence swallows the room.

It isn't until the front door opens and closes a few seconds later that she finally looks up.

"You've got to be kidding me," she says, shaking her head, her gaze shifting from me to Wes. "Is Jase going to walk in any second, too?"

Wes ignores her, his attention focused on me. "You get here in time?"

"False alarm," I tell him. "It was Jimmy the photographer. He's making breakfast."

"Jimmy the photographer," Wes repeats, frowning, and I nearly laugh. He looks just as confused as I felt when she first told me who was here.

"Yes," Piper snaps, and she points to Jimmy, who's still standing in the kitchen doorway watching us curiously. "That's Jimmy. He's a photographer. He's also a friend of mine. What is so hard to understand about this?"

"It's five in the morning, babe," Wes says seriously. "You usually work until one, and then sleep until nine-thirty. You don't get visitors at five in the morning."

"How do you even know that?" she asks, and then right away she shakes her head and says, "Never mind. I don't want to know."

Wes regards her for a moment, before shifting his hard gaze to Jimmy. "What the fuck are you doing sneaking around her house at five o'clock in the goddamn morning?"

Jimmy cringes. "My ex changed the locks on me, and then

when I got here, I found that Piper did the same." He frowns, shaking his head. "It really hasn't been a good night."

"You and Tara broke up?" Piper asks, swinging her now worried gaze to him.

"I emailed you about ..." he stalls, stuffing his hands in his pockets. "Right, I didn't send you that email either. Okay, long story short, I met someone else. She's perfect. She's amazing. She's a photographer, too. As soon as I met her, I just knew, you know? I knew she's what I've been missing, so I broke it off with Tara before I left for Denver because it wouldn't be cool to stay with her when I have these feelings for someone else. I thought she was cool with it, but she locked me out so I'm guessing she's not."

Piper stares at him for a moment, with what looks like pity. She opens her mouth to say something, but stops herself, turning to look at me. "You should probably go before you're late."

"Late for what?" Wes asks, once more sounding confused. "I thought Jimmy was making breakfast."

I hesitate, contemplating how to respond to that, wondering if I should humor Piper and play along since she really doesn't seem to want us to stick around.

"He is," I say, "but we can't stay. We've got that meeting."

Wes shakes his head, smiles at Piper, and then not missing a beat, he says, "Right, I forgot about that. I'll meet you at Heaven Here in twenty, yeah?"

"I'm right behind you," I say, "but the meeting is at Sunnyside."

Wes laughs. "Right. Sunnyside Eatery, five-thirty. Got it."

I roll my eyes, and he laughs again, before saying a quick goodbye to Piper and walking out the door.

She smiles at me when he leaves, mouthing a silent *thank you*, and for a second, I'm struck by the sight. She's so damn pretty. Even just waking up, her hair knotted and disheveled, she's pretty.

For a second, I find myself wondering why I've never asked her out before, but it's a senseless thought, because I know the answer. She's Kim's best friend and that could've been awkward and messy with them living together, and she also had a man for most of the time I've known her.

But she doesn't have a man now.

She hasn't for six months.

And she hasn't lived with Kim for six months either.

"Have dinner with me tonight," I say.

Her eyes widen, but she doesn't hesitate, doesn't even take a second to consider it, shaking her head quickly. "Um ... I can't," she says. "I have plans."

My eyebrows raise at her quick shut down, my expression no doubt betraying my shock.

Well, shit. I thought she'd at least consider it.

"Kim and I are going out for drinks," she blurts suddenly, as though she feels the need to explain. "Girl's night."

The corner of my mouth turns up in a half smile, and then it spreads into a full-blown grin. "Then have dinner with me tomorrow."

"I, uh ... I don't know if that's a good idea," she says. "I'm kind of behind with work right now."

She's right, it's probably not a good idea, but I'm not sure I care about that anymore.

Reaching over, I cup her chin, tilting her head up to look at me. I can see raw vulnerability in her eyes. "It's just dinner. Work or not, you've still gotta eat."

"I know, but ..."

"I'll pick you up at seven, honey," I say, stopping her before she can make up another excuse.

Pink tints her cheeks as she rolls her eyes and she nods, a small smile on her lips. "Okay."

I smile, brushing my thumb over her bottom lip, before letting my hand fall away. "I'll see you tomorrow, Piper," I say, and then I walk out the door to go meet Wes for breakfast.

Chapter Four

Piper

"Okay, I'm confused," Kim says, wrinkling her nose overdramatically as she comes back from the kitchen, handing me a fresh beer. "Why is Jimmy staying here?"

"Out of everything I've told you, that's what you're confused about?" I ask and laugh, before taking a deep sip from my drink.

It's nearly six o'clock, and we're both well on our way to a happy buzzed place. She got here about an hour ago and I've been filling her in on what I've dubbed the *Vance Conundrum* ever since.

She sat and listened as I told her about the crazy alarm system he installed, and the lecture I received from the guys yesterday about not already having one.

She giggled when I told her about Jimmy showing up here this morning, and then she full out laughed when I told her about Vance and Wes showing up shortly after and that Vance kept a key to my house.

Then she squealed when I informed her that I now have a dinner date tomorrow night.

But other than the sound effects, she didn't make a single comment as I filled her in, only stopping me to refill her margarita, and now that I'm done, the only thing that's confusing her is Jimmy?

"Well, yeah," she says, giving me an odd look as she drops down unceremoniously beside me on the couch, propping her feet up on the coffee table. She takes a dainty sip of her drink, and sighs, before continuing, "Vance monitoring your alarm and keeping a key to your house isn't confusing. He did the same for our apartment. And as for going to dinner, all I can say about that is it's about damn time he made a move. He's had a thing for you for years. But Jimmy ... that's confusing."

Wait ... what?

I cock my head. "He's had a thing for me for years?"

Kim snorts back a laugh, waving her strawberry margarita in my direction. "Are you kidding me? It was so obvious. The way he watched you anytime he came around and the way he always glared at Colton like he was a bug that needed to be stomped on. He's wanted your attention since he met you."

I consider this for a moment, wondering how I never noticed, but it's a senseless thought. I know why. I was too nervous around him, too busy trying to pretend I didn't notice him to notice he was noticing me. Grandma Owen always said I was oblivious to boys, too. Maybe I need to pull my head out of my ass more often and notice what's going on around me.

"Huh," I say finally, slightly reluctantly. "Okay, I guess maybe it was kind of obvious."

"Vance isn't going to like Jimmy staying here," Kim says seriously. "He should go to a hotel or stay with a friend."

"I am a friend," I point out, raising an eyebrow. "And it's really none of Vance's business. Jimmy can stay here as long as he needs."

Speaking of Jimmy ...

My eyes shift to him as he walks into the living room and sits down in the recliner, a beer in hand. He takes a gulp of his drink as he leans back, popping out the leg rest on the chair.

"Thanks for letting me use your office," he says once he's settled.

"Not a problem," I say. "Did you get everything you needed done?"

"Yep," he says, taking another sip of his beer, before he cuts his eyes to me again. "So I was thinking about this situation you have and I've come to the conclusion that the person that's been vandalizing your place has to be a woman."

Kim looks at me with a blank face, and when I only shrug, she turns the same expression on Jimmy. "How do you figure that?"

Jimmy shrugs a shoulder, and takes another pull from his beer. "Most men wouldn't bother with chopping up rose bushes or spray painting vague warnings on garage doors. They'd take a more direct route to get the message across. A man would actually tell you what the message is. This petty shit just feels like a woman's behind it."

"I think I should be offended," I say, and Kim laughs at me.

"As much as I hate to admit it, he's probably right," she says. "This whole thing feels like a woman with a grudge, but what about the brick through the window? That has to have been a man."

Jimmy shakes his head. "The person broke the window, but didn't try to get in, right?"

I nod. "Yeah, that's right."

"It's a woman," he says. "A man probably would have taken it a step further, but by that point he would have already warned you off, so you wouldn't be guessing who was messing with you, you'd know."

I open my mouth to protest, because his reasoning, although for the most part makes sense, also sounds absurd, but Kim holds up a hand, stopping me, her expression uncharacteristically serious.

"I'm not sure I get where you're going with the whole window breaking part," she says. "If it's a man, he could just be trying to scare her, but the rest of it ..." she stalls, frowning. "When you think about it, it does seem like a woman, doesn't it?"

"So you both think it's a woman?" I ask, my eyes darting between them.

Kim nods, and Jimmy shrugs.

"You need to make a list," Jimmy says. "Write down all the

women you've pissed off since moving to Sacramento."

Ugh. I hate making lists.

I take another long pull of beer, finishing off the bottle, and then sigh dramatically as I set the empty bottle on the table. "Okay, I'll make a list, but I need another beer first and we definitely need to order pizza."

Kim rolls her eyes unsympathetically. "Look on the positive side," she says. "We've ruled out all the men you've pissed off over the years. We're making progress."

We order pizza, Hawaiian for me with extra pineapple, pepperoni for Kim, and a meat lovers for Jimmy, and then we get to work, making the list.

Two and a half hours later, I'm full and in a happy buzzed place, and the list is almost finished. It isn't long, only a handful of names. We probably would have finished it sooner if we hadn't decided to write down the entire story of why each person was a suspect, including motives and their *Piper Hatred* levels using a scale of one to ten, but at least it made it somewhat interesting.

Tapping my pen against the coffee table as I read over the list, I consider scratching off Heather Tane's name. Is ordering the last large cup of coffee really a motive to trash my rose bushes? Yeah, she was annoyed and she did call me a bitch, but Heather is always annoyed and she calls everyone a bitch, and besides that, it really wasn't my fault the shop ran out of large cups, right?

"Okay, this is getting boring," Kim says, gulping down her margarita and standing up. "Let's go to Constant Pub. We can get dressed up, go dancing, have some fun."

"Hell yeah," Jimmy says. "I love Constant Pub. It's got good people there and the drinks are cheap."

I shake my head. "Constant Pub isn't really a place for dancing."

"Any place with music is a place for dancing," Kim counters, her voice serious.

"I don't think so," I say, shaking my head again. "We should stay here and do a whole stake out thing, watch the monitors for the jerk to come back and catch her. Besides, we've already been drinking and I hate cabs."

Kim pouts, full on, droopy lip, pouts. "That sounds just as boring as making a list. Jimmy only had one beer so he can drive us, and Vance is watching the house. He'll catch her if she shows up again."

This is true.

There's really no point in both of us watching, right? And we've already made progress. We ruled out men ... We made a list ...

"Come on, Pipes," Kim whines. "It's Friday night. Live a little."

"Okay, let's go out," I say, deciding that I might as well let go for the night and have some fun.

Kim and I make a crash stop in my bedroom, tearing through my closet, throwing clothes around, searching for something to wear. We pull shirts off hangers, holding them up, before tossing them aside.

It takes about fifteen minutes, but Kim finally settles on a little black dress, while I pull on a slinky green sleeveless top that dips low with a cowl neck at the front, and a pair of black skinny jeans.

Letting my hair out of its braid, I run my fingers through the waves, fluffing it out. I swipe on some lip-gloss and blush, before slipping on a pair of sling back, peep-toed sandals, and then, Jimmy, Kim, and I hop into my truck and head to the pub.

It's a twenty-minute drive to the pub and Jimmy yammers on about the new girl, Sera, the entire way. By the time we get there, I know she's twenty-one, blonde, blue eyed, has a dog named Killer and a cat named Puss. She works at a photo hut and they met when he went in to buy film for his camera.

The parking lot is packed when we pull in, and I swear we find the last parking spot.

There's a small group of men standing at the entrance, smoking and laughing with the bouncer. He eyes us for a moment as we approach before recognition settles in and he lifts his chin, letting us in without any hassle.

The bar is just as packed as the parking lot with people chatting and laughing, the atmosphere and crowd, relaxed, easy, with low music thrumming through the air.

It's always like this here. It's one of the things I love about this place.

Jimmy goes straight for the bar, squeezing through the crowd, and stands at the end, waiting for the bartender to notice him, and Kim and I start the hunt for a table.

"Oh, look," Kim says, pointing to a table near the bar. "It's Vance and Wes."

I turn, seeing Vance staring at us, his expression blank. He makes a show of running his eyes over me, his attention causing a tingle to shoot down my spine. I'm not sure if it's from excitement or apprehension, until he meets my eyes, smiles, and then lifts a hand waving us over, and I realize it's both.

I'm excited he's here.

I'm nervous to see him again.

It hits me then, Friday night, Constant Pub ... Vance comes here almost every Friday night.

I turn to Kim, narrowing my eyes at her. "You knew he'd be here tonight, didn't you?"

"No," she says right away, except she's also nodding yes.

"I thought this was supposed to be a girl's night," I say.

Kim lets out a sharp laugh. "Jimmy ruined that, not me."

I bite my bottom lip, and my emotions must be easy to see because Kim giggles.

"Nervous is good," she fake whispers, over the music. "If you're not nervous about seeing him, then you're just not that into him." Then, before I can respond, she grabs my hand, tugging me toward the table. "Come on."

I follow her, although I really don't have much of a choice. Her grip on my arm is bruising tight. She's not taking any chances that I'll chicken out and find another table.

Vance watches me intently as we make our way over, and even slightly intoxicated, the attention flusters me. Wearing his standard uniform of faded jeans, a dark tee, and a baseball cap, he looks good.

Really good.

"Hey guys," Kim says brightly as we reach the table. She moves in behind Vance, wrapping her arms around his neck, and plants a kiss on his cheek, and then moves on to Wes, repeating the routine, before taking a seat.

"Someone's drunk," Vance says, amusement passing across his face as he eyes his cousin.

"Not drunk," Kim says, grinning at him. "Happily buzzed."

Vance shakes his head slowly and smiles, as he tugs out the chair beside him, gesturing for me to sit. "Thought you were out on a girl's night."

I slip into the chair. "Me, too."

Vance shakes his head again, this time at me, and he smiles. "Glad that girl's night brought you here. You want a drink?"

I shake my head. "Jimmy's getting them, but thanks."

"Jimmy's here, too?" He raises his eyebrows questioningly. "On girl's night?"

I roll my eyes. "He is staying with me. It's not like I could just leave him out, and he did save me from having to take a cab here so it's all good."

His brow furrows, his eyes turning dark and hard. "So he's staying with you now?"

Crap.

That's not a happy look. Not happy at all.

Quickly, I consider how to respond, wondering if somehow I can just avoid this conversation all together. I glance at Kim, quickly catching her eye, and she gives me a look that clearly says, *I told you so.*

I can feel Vance's attention on me, waiting for my response. It unnerves me on so many levels that I can't even begin to pinpoint how I feel about his unhappiness. My stomach flutters while another sensation desperately tries to snuff it out.

Frustration.

But then Kim smiles, winking at me.

"Where's Jase?" Kim asks, reaching across the table, and nabs Vance's beer, drawing his attention. She takes a sip and makes a sour face. "That's just gross."

I smile inwardly. God, I love my best friend.

"Jase is at home," Vance says, rolling his eyes as he snags his beer back. "He's Skyping with Elena again."

"When's she coming back?" Kim asks. "I'm dying to meet the girl that has Jason Pierce missing Friday night drinks to sit at a computer."

"Supposed to be Wednesday, but it's been put off again," Wes says. "She just bought a truck and is gonna drive back now, leaving New York on Thursday."

"Ooo, another truck girl," Kim says, winking at me. "Nice."

Jimmy appears at the table, his hands wrapped around a beer, a bottled water, and some pink concoction. "Piper's beer, my water, and Kim's summer breeze," he says, passing out the drinks. "Next time, let the guy that's buying you drinks know where you're going."

Kim giggles. "I knew you'd find us."

Thanking Jimmy for the drink, I reach for it, taking a sip, as Kim starts rambling on about the list we made, explaining to Vance and Wes why it has to be a woman that's been messing with me.

They talk.

They laugh.

They drink some more.

Ten minutes passes … fifteen minutes … and I think I'm in the clear. Thanks to Kim I've managed avoidance, but then, Vance leans into me. "You do know I caught that whole *distract Vance* look you shared with Kim, yeah?"

"Yep," I say. "But tonight I'm just trying to have fun with some friends. I don't want to worry about your issues with Jimmy staying with me, because news flash, we haven't even had our first date, so please just drop it for tonight."

He flinches at my sharp tone and leans back in his chair.

Crap. That came out wrong, too blunt and too harsh.

Ugh. Too much stress and alcohol is totally to blame here.

He eyes me peculiarly, as though trying to decide whether or not to accept my words. I open my mouth, about to tell him that I didn't mean it the way it came out, but he must see it in my expression because he tugs me into his side, wrapping an arm around me. Bringing his lips close to my ear, he says, "I've just got one question for you."

"Sure," I say, feeling my stomach sink with dread. *Please don't let it be something serious. Please ...*

"You and Jimmy seem close," he says. "Should I be worried about that?"

A bark of laughter escapes me before I can swallow it down. Worried about Jimmy? I think that's the funniest thing I've heard all night.

Shaking my head, I meet his eyes, still laughing. "Trust me," I say. "You do not have to worry about that."

Chapter Five

Vance

An hour creeps by and the girls have officially gone past *happily buzzed* to wasted.

They joke around, drinking and laughing.

Piper eventually loosens up.

I mull over their new theory on who's been harassing her in silence.

Jimmy starts doing shots.

I switch to water.

I've come to the conclusion that the person is most likely watching Piper, although I know she won't admit that. She doesn't like the thought of a stalker, or maybe it's just the word. I'm not really sure.

What I am sure about is that for ten days straight, something has happened, and then yesterday after an alarm system is installed, nothing.

It's possible that it's just a coincidence, but it's also possible the person was watching, saw us put it in, and decided to regroup.

It's the latter that feels right to me. Ten days is a long time to mess with someone to just … forget about it and move on. And the *stay away* warning that was spray painted on her garage tells me this is personal.

She probably knows the person.

She's most likely wronged them in some way.

I check my phone again, ensuring it's still on and I haven't missed anything. The bar is loud; people are getting rowdy, their voices rising, and their laughter louder as more drinks are served. It would be easy to miss an alert in here, but with another glance at the security app, I find her house dark and quiet.

"What are you looking at?" Piper asks, leaning into me, resting a hand on my thigh as she peeks at my phone.

My eyes shift to her, scanning her in the dim light. "Your house."

Piper tenses and she pulls her hand away from my thigh, bringing it to her mouth. "Oh, no. Did something happen?"

"No," I say. "Everything's fine."

She sags back into me instantly, a small smile appearing on her face. It's relief, I think, but there's still a trace of uncertainty in her eyes. "Can I see?"

Holding my phone so she can see, I tap on the screen, first pulling up the front of the house, the garage, and then the back, showing her that everything's fine.

She's silent for a moment, staring at the phone, before she shifts her gaze to me, eyeing me warily. "I told you I didn't want you looking into this for me," she says, sounding somewhat annoyed, but her hand comes back to my thigh.

My eyes leave hers momentarily distracted, and they settle on her hand. Her small hand, palm down; her slim fingers slightly squeezing the muscle there. I bring my hand down to hers, entwining our fingers. It feels so natural, and for the second time today, I find myself wondering why it's taken her needing help for me to finally make a move.

It strikes me then, a feeling of loss.

I wasted so much time.

Missed so much.

I blow out a dismissive breath, but whether it's to the comment or the feeling, I'm not entirely sure. "You knew I wouldn't listen."

"It's kind of creepy," she says, reaching over with her free hand, tapping the screen and closing the app.

My brow furrows. "What's creepy?"

"With just a couple taps on your phone, you can watch my house any time you want," she says. "It's kind of creepy."

I put my phone away, glancing at her, seeing an unexpected look of curiosity on her face. Before I can respond, however, Kim chimes in. "She's right. It's creepy."

I roll my eyes. "It's not creepy, it's security."

"Nope," Wes says, his shoulders shaking with silent laughter. "It's definitely creepy. Maybe I should watch the house instead."

I cock a brow. "How is that any different?"

"Because he's not trying to, uh ... date me," Piper says, blushing.

Regarding her curiously, I ask, "Do you want Wes or Jase to watch the house instead of me?"

Piper wavers, pondering my question, before she wrinkles her nose and shakes her head. "Nope. I'm okay with you being kind of creepy."

I let out a sharp bark of laughter. "Good to know."

Shaking her head and snorting out a laugh, she takes another small sip of her beer. The banter starts up again, flowing freely between Kim and Piper, and Jimmy heads to the bar for another round.

It's then that I notice her again. A woman, young, face caked with make-up, short blonde hair, bright blue eyes ... It's the sixth, maybe seventh time she's walked by our table, staring at the girls as she passes, making her way to the bar.

Wes notices her, too.

He glances at me, frowning, before turning his eyes back to her, watching as her head swivels, her hard gaze staying on our table, as she slips past us.

It's not until she's well past, that she diverts her attention to the bar, saddling up beside Jimmy. She says something to him, and he jerks in surprise.

He doesn't looked thrilled to see her.

Actually, he almost looks like a cornered animal.

I turn to Piper, and I'm about to ask if either of them knows the woman, when suddenly Piper squeals, hopping in her chair, and a smile lights up her face. It's the kind of smile that could replace sunshine. "I love this song," she says, shoving her chair back and jumping up. "Kimmy, dance with me."

Kim laughs. "I thought you said Constant Pub isn't really a place for dancing."

"And you said any place with music is a place for dancing," she counters, shaking her ass. "Come on."

Kim doesn't take much more coaxing. A few whiny pleas and another bright smile from Piper, and she's up, teetering on her feet, yelling toward the bar, "Turn that jam up!"

From behind the bar, Sam glances up, spots the girls moving into the aisle, only a few steps from our table, shaking their hips as they go, and he obliges, cranking up the tune.

I don't know the song. It's some pop/hip-hop crap, but then Piper starts to move, and I couldn't care less what kind of music it is because she loves it. I can see it on her face, feel it in the way she dances.

She twirls. She shimmies. She throws her hands in the air and sings along, belting out the lyrics.

She isn't trying to be sexy or draw attention, but I swear, every head turns, drawn to her as she moves.

She looks so … *carefree*.

I stare at her, my gaze slowly raking down her body, reaching her toes, before trailing back up. Her hips sway to the beat, all her curves proudly on display. Confidence seems to ooze from her pores, bordering on downright cocky. Maybe it's the booze, or maybe she's just having fun. I'm not entirely sure, but this isn't the shy girl I've gotten to know over the last few years, or even the one I saw this morning.

This is a girl letting go, a girl having fun.

She's laughing with Kim, smiling so big that it looks painful.

So damn pretty.

I think I could watch her dance like this, smile like this, for hours, days even.

But then the song ends and instant disappointment hits me,

settling deep in my gut as Piper stops moving.

"Play it again," I say. "Someone needs to play that song again." The words are out of my mouth and in the air before I have enough sense to restrain them or even realize what I'm saying.

I glance at Wes, hoping like hell he didn't hear me, because Jesus, who says something like that? But he did. He heard me. I can see the amusement flash in his eyes. He's silent for a tick, regarding me peculiarly, and then he throws his head back and laughs. Hard. So hard he nearly falls off his chair. The animated sound draws the girls' attention, and they make their way back to the table, only a few short strides.

Kim's eyes flicker to me before focusing on Wes. Quirking a brow, she asks, "What's so funny?"

"Play it again," Wes chokes out, laughing harder.

Piper's brow furrows, looking at me. "What's he talking about?"

I cut my eyes at Wes, feigning irritation, before letting out a rueful laugh and glancing back at Piper. "I *might* have been disappointed that the song ended and you stopped dancing, and I *might* have expressed that I wanted someone to play it again."

"Oh," Piper half whispers, looking away bashfully. It doesn't escape my notice that her cheeks flush.

She opens her mouth to say something else, but doesn't get the chance, because Jimmy is suddenly there, throwing his arm over her shoulder. "Come on, Pipes. Time to get out of here."

Piper

"Jimmy, let go," I say, trying to push my way out of his grasp. "What's wrong with you?"

He doesn't let go, dragging me out of the bar, into the parking lot. "Tara's here," he says. "She's pissed, we had words, and we need to go before I get tossed out."

"What do you mean you had words?" I ask incredulously, digging my heels in, trying to get him to stop, but only succeeding in making myself stumble in my sandals.

He steadies me quickly, not slowing down, and pulls the keys to my truck out of his pocket. "Just trust me, we need to go."

He only makes it another step before Vance and Wes catch up to us, cutting in front of him, and Jimmy comes to a sudden stop, letting me go instantly.

"You're not driving her anywhere." Vance's voice is low and menacing, and he snatches the keys out of Jimmy's hand.

"Hey." Jimmy reaches for the keys. "Give those back."

Vance merely holds them higher, shaking his head. "You've been doing shots for the last forty minutes."

"Fine, whatever," Jimmy says, dropping his hands. "But I need to get out of here."

Wes folds his arms over his chest, looking pissed off. "This have anything to do with the young blonde at the bar?"

Jimmy nods. "She's my ex. It got ugly, she said some things, I said some things, and then the bartender told me to get out or he'd have me escorted out and he'd call the cops."

"What did you say to her?" Kim asks, catching up to us, her tone stern.

Jimmy shakes his head. "It doesn't matter. We just have to go."

Vance narrows his eyes and his teeth clench.

"We'll call a cab," I say, reluctantly, not liking the idea. I'm really not a fan of letting someone I don't know drive me around. It's like putting my life in the hands of a stranger.

But Jimmy's supposed to be our driver, and if he's been doing shots, then he's just as unsafe to drive with as a cabby.

"No, I'll take you," Vance says, as he digs into his pocket. He pulls out his keys and tosses them to Wes. "You mind taking Kim home, and then picking me up at Piper's?"

Wes catches the keys. "I'm on it."

Kim grins, looking from Vance to me curiously, before she links her arm through Jimmy's. "Come on, dumbass," she says. "You can stay with me tonight."

I start to protest, but Kim won't hear it. She quickly says goodbye, making me promise to call her as soon as I wake up, and then the three of them take off toward Vance's truck, and Vance leads me to mine.

Opening the door for me, Vance helps me climb up, giving me a little boost, before shutting me in. I toss my purse in the back of the cab, and then clip my seatbelt, as Vance comes around to the driver's side, hops in, and starts it up. He then backs out of the parking space and pulls out of the lot.

We drive in comfortable silence for a few minutes, and my nerves for once don't make an appearance. I think it's the alcohol mixed with exhaustion, making me feel so at ease.

"I had fun tonight," I say, breaking the silence. "Thanks for driving me home." My voice comes out scratchy and dry, and I lean back, shoving my hand through the seat feeling around for my purse. I bet I have some mints in there or gum.

Vance steals a quick glance at me and smiles, before turning his eyes back to the road. "I had fun, too."

Silence falls once more.

I keep reaching around, straining my arm, tapping my hand along the floor. God, my throat feels so dry it hurts.

Where is that purse?

"What are you doing?" Vance asks.

"Looking for my purse."

Giving up on the blind hand search, I unclasp my seatbelt and turn around, leaning into the back of the cab, looking around for it.

"Jesus Christ, Piper," Vance says, his hand landing on my hip as though to keep me steady. "Sit down and put your seatbelt on. You can grab your purse when I get you home."

"But I ..." I start, but stop as an odd rattling, clanking sound hits my ears, and Vance lets out a stream of curses. I feel him touching the brakes, small little jerks, as though he's trying to slow down, but careful not to slam them on with me not wearing a seatbelt.

"Piper, seatbelt, now," Vance says, cutting me off. His voice has an edge to it, one I've never heard from him before, not even when he's stressing about Kim. He sounds ... anxious? Maybe calm, too. Whatever it is, it's unnerving.

I start to shuffle back, but I guess I'm not moving fast enough, because he grips the waist of my jeans, tugging me back into my seat, and then reaches across me, holding me in place.

Then he hits the brakes, telling me to hold on, and then the truck is bouncing, and we're sliding, tipping, jerking. My head hits the window, smashing hard enough that I hear the glass crack. Time stands still for what seems like minutes, though I'm sure it's only seconds, and then the truck flips, and everything goes dark.

Chapter Six

Vance

Time moves in a blur. Mere seconds pass, but it feels like an eternity as the truck tips over and crashes onto the pavement. The driver's side window shatters as it hits the ground, the glass exploding inward, raining against the side of my face in a million tiny shards. Piper jerks forward, wrenching at my arm as I struggle to keep her in her seat.

Pain snaps through my wrist, shooting up my elbow and into my shoulder. My grip on her begins to slip and panic that I'm going to drop her stalks around the edges of my mind, but I refuse to let it in.

Inhaling through my mouth and exhaling through my nose, I try to breathe through the pain, and I tighten my hold on her, pressing my forearm more snuggly against her chest and digging my elbow into the seat beside her, holding her up, so she doesn't come tumbling into me.

The truck shudders, the metal frame protesting this new, foreign position, and then everything goes quiet and still, only the calm idle of the engine remaining.

For a beat, all I can do is sit here, unmoving, unbreathing, one hand gripping the steering wheel, and the other pressed against Piper's chest.

My mind works fast trying to put all the pieces together. The rattle, the shaking, a tire flying in the rearview mirror, the truck bouncing, the rotor hitting the ground, catching, tipping …

When my lungs finally manage an in and out again, I blow out a long breath, ending it with the word, "Fuck."

And then, I turn to look at Piper.

Her head is down, her face hidden from my view, and she's breathing hard, her pulse hammering against my forearm, but her body is slack, pressed tight against the center console, and folding itself over my arm.

"Piper," I say, my voice rough. "You okay, honey?"

She doesn't respond.

Not even a whisper.

"Piper," I try again, louder this time.

Again, no response.

Heart pounding, my panic kicks up once more and it's all I can do to wrangle it and push it down. I shift in my seat, careful not to let her go. Shards of glass dig into my hand as I press it against the window frame, turning my body toward her.

Something warm and wet trickles onto my forearm as I move, and my eyes slice to it.

Blood. Oh shit, it's blood.

I lean up toward her, my eyes frantically scanning, searching for the source. The right side of her face is covered in it, sliding down her cheek from her hairline.

My chest tightens, suddenly feeling as though it's engulfed in flames, and another curse leaves my lips on a sharp exhale.

I stare at it.

A second passes.

Two.

And then I move into action.

Changing my grip on her, I wind my arm around her, getting a more secure hold, and then I reach my free arm in between us, hitting the release on my seatbelt, moving closer to her, needing to see the rise and fall of her chest, the proof that she's alive.

She jostles in my arm, eliciting a sudden gasp and sob from her lips that sends ice running down my spine.

"Freckles, talk to me," I say, bringing my hand up to cup her bloodied cheek, tilting her face up, so I can get a better look at her. "Open those eyes."

She gasps again, followed by another quick sob and a loud groan, and then her eyes open. She blinks a few times, her eyelashes fluttering rapidly, and then she tilts her head back, looking at me.

"Did you just call me freckles?" she rasps, scrunching her nose. Her expression might be comical, if I wasn't so goddamn worried.

"Yeah," I say, my voice harsh with unease. "I did."

She eyes me peculiarly, her nose scrunching once more, the movement of her face causing more blood to slide down her cheek and run over my hand.

She feels it. I see it in her eyes, a flutter of confusion, and then realization settling in their depths.

"Oh, God, am I ...?" she stalls, her shaky hand flying up to her cheek, pressing against mine. "Is that ...?"

Piper's face pales as she pulls her hand away, staring at the blood staining her palm and fingers. Her lips begin to tremble, her breath hitches, her hand shakes.

"Don't think about it," I say quickly, pushing her hand down out of her line of sight. "You're fine."

And she is fine.

She's breathing.

She's talking.

That's good, right?

Head injuries bleed a lot. It's probably not as bad as it looks. It can't be.

She eyes me dubiously for a tick, her gaze flickering down to her hand once, twice, three times, before she blows out a shaky breath. "Are you o-okay?"

I nod once. "Yeah, I'm good."

"W-what happened?" she stammers out, her voice borderline panicked, her eyes wide with fear, as she scans them over me, searchingly, as though she's not sure she should believe that I'm good.

"Rear driver's side tire came off," I say.

"You mean we got a flat?" she asks, frowning, as she presses her arm against the center console, taking some of her weight off me. "A flat tire flipped the truck?"

"No, Piper," I respond, my tone, just as disbelieving as hers. "The rim, the tire, it all came off."

She stares at me, a mix of muddled skepticism and blatant alarm flitting across her face. She doesn't want to believe me. I don't blame her for that. It's not like a tire, rim and all, flies off vehicles every day.

"We've gotta get you out of here so I can look at you," I say, my gaze shifting past her, scanning over the door at her back. "The door is gonna be hard to keep open, so I'm gonna open your window, and you're gonna need to climb out. You think you can do that?"

She nods, wincing from the movement. "Yeah, I think I can do that."

I reach behind me, feeling around for the button, not taking my eyes off her. After a moment of searching, my finger hits the button, and I press down, allowing the window to slide open.

"You ready?" I ask.

Piper nods again. "Yeah."

"Okay," I say. "Grab onto the window frame and climb out. I'll give you a boost, yeah?"

She gives me a wobbly, watery smile and another nod, before she swivels in the seat and leans up, grasping the window frame with both hands, and hoists herself up. Shifting positions, I move my hands to her hips, grimacing at the stab of pain that cuts through my wrist as I give her a boost.

Shit. I think it's sprained.

The truck groans and rocks as Piper scrambles out, nearly kicking me in the face as she goes, but I manage to avoid her flailing limbs. Her feet disappear from my view, and then the truck settles again as she hops down, the soles of her shoes clacking against the pavement.

Once she's clear, I maneuver myself out of my seat, crouching on the shattered remains of the window. As I rise, I spot Piper's purse in the corner of the back seat and I snag it, before standing and pulling myself out the window.

When my feet hit the ground, Piper is on her ass on the pavement. She's leaning against the roof of the truck, with her arms wrapped around her shins, her forehead pressed against her knees, and her body shaking ever so slightly.

Clutching her purse, I move to her quickly, squatting down in front of her. "You doing okay?" I ask, reaching out a hand, and grasping her shoulder gently.

Slowly, she lifts her head and her voice is scratchy as she says, "Yeah, just dizzy. A little queasy, too. I think I drank too much."

I snort out an unamused laugh. I doubt the dizziness and queasiness has little to do with the alcohol she consumed tonight.

"Let me get a look at you," I say, setting her purse down beside her and cupping her chin in my hand. She winces as I tilt her head to the side, and she cringes as I poke and prod at her hair, looking for the source of all the blood.

The gash isn't too long, or too deep, about an inch, maybe an inch and a half above her ear on the right side of her head.

"Is it bad?" she asks, a slight tremor coming through in her voice.

I shake my head. "No, but you're gonna need a few stitches and we've gotta slow down the bleeding."

Piper grimaces, but she doesn't say anything. I wonder if it's the thought of stitches or the blood that makes her cheeks pale further.

I glance around for something to use to stop the flow of blood, thinking perhaps there's something in the truck—a towel, a shirt, something—but a snap second decision has me pulling off my tee, bunching it up, and pressing it against the side of her head.

"Ouch," Piper whines, wincing away from the pressure. She reaches up, batting away my hand, and takes the tee, pressing it to her head nowhere near as firmly as I had it.

"Hold it tight," I say, cupping her hand in mine, applying more pressure. "Just like this, yeah? I'm gonna call this in."

"Okay," she says, her voice shaking over the word.

With another thorough scan of her, making sure she doesn't let up on the pressure, I pull my phone out of my pocket, taking a couple steps back as I dial 9-1-1, quickly rambling off our location and reporting the accident to the operator. I describe Piper's injury, saying we need police, paramedics, and a tow truck.

The operator bombards me with a ton of questions. Is she still bleeding? Is she awake? Did she lose consciousness? How long was she out? Has she vomited? I answer the questions, my tone crisp and concise, and my patience nears its snapping point as she keeps firing them at me.

I want to get off the phone.

I need to focus on Piper.

Where the fuck is the ambulance?

Suddenly, Piper makes a noise, a mix of a groan and a whimper, and I whip my gaze back to her. She meets my eyes, and my chest tightens at the distress I see swimming there. "Gonna be sick," she gasps, sniveling. "Gonna be sick."

"Gotta put the phone down," I bark out, darting back to Piper's side, and setting the phone down on the pavement. I manage to pull her hair back from her face, and grab the tee before it falls from her wound, just as Piper vomits onto the ground beside her.

My gut clenches, unease and concern twisting me in knots, as her body shakes and convulses through wave after wave of sickness.

When she stops heaving, she just sits there, staring down at the ground. "Thanks for holding my hair," she mumbles, her voice barely a whisper.

"Do you think you're gonna be sick again?" I ask gently.

"Feeling a little better now," she says, reaching up and taking hold of the tee again.

"Okay," I say with a nod, eyeing the puddle of vomit. "Let's get you moved then."

The sounds of sirens ring out in the distance, so I don't bother to pick up the phone again. Instead, I scoop up Piper, cradling her against my chest, and stride over to the curb, well away from where she was just sick, and I take a seat, keeping her in my lap.

"Police are close," she says, shivering and burrowing into me, as though seeking my warmth.

"Yeah," I respond, wrapping my arms around her shoulders. Fuck, I hate seeing her like this, hate not being able to do more to make her feel better.

A bucket of rage settles itself in my chest. *Goddamnit!* She shouldn't have even been hurt in the first place.

I should have pulled over quicker.

I should have held onto her tighter.

I should have …

"H-how did the tire come off?" she asks.

I hesitate, considering her question, contemplating how to answer. I want to tell her shit happens, that it was an accident and nothing more, but the thing is, tires don't just fly off vehicles. The bolts don't just miraculously come loose. My gut is telling me someone tampered with her truck.

Someone loosened the bolts.

More goddamn vandalism.

Except this is different.

This isn't just some ruined rose bushes or spray paint.

This is serious.

Someone wanted to hurt her. But who? And why?

I don't have a goddamn clue.

I shake away the thoughts and the questions swarming my brain. There will be time to take apart everything that happened tonight, examine it, look at it piece by piece, later.

I cut my eyes to her, seeing her inquisitive expression marred with worry, and I mutter, "I don't know, honey, but I promise you, I'll find out."

Her expression softens, the concentration and sickness melting from her features. "Freckles," she says. "I like freckles better. It's more personal, not so generic."

Despite myself, I chuckle, hugging her in closer. "Freckles it is then."

She stares at me for a tick, her expression turning contemplative once more.

"What are you thinking so hard about?" I ask.

"I need a good name for you," she says seriously. "You know something like freckles, but for you."

It's probably the alcohol still swimming in her system, but she looks so goddamn serious, as though we're discussing politics or religion or some life and death situation, that I nearly laugh again.

"I like the one you already have for me," I say, fighting to keep my tone just as serious as hers.

She lifts an eyebrow questioningly, looking thoroughly confused.

"Badass hottie," I say, feeling my lips quirk up as laughter bubbles up my throat. "It has a nice ring to it."

Piper rolls her eyes, and I laugh.

"Bring that up again and I'll start calling you ..." she purses her lips, frowning in concentration, before huffing out a dramatic breath. "Well I don't really know yet, but you won't like it."

Piper

The next hour and a half passes by in a haze with my truck being towed, me giving a statement to the police officers while the paramedics check me over, being taken and admitted to the hospital, and getting stitches—five to be exact, right above my ear—all the while dealing with the lingering and not so pleasant effects of the alcohol I'd consumed earlier and trying (and failing) to wrap my head around how exactly my tire had fallen off.

By the time I'm discharged from the hospital, my hangover is kicking in with a vengeance, leaving me feeling clammy, shaky, and a whole lot like I've been run over by a truck.

Walking slowly, Vance guides me out to the parking lot where Jase and Wes are waiting. His right hand, along with his wrist and forearm, is wrapped in a tensor bandage. He sprained it from trying to keep me in my seat. He keeps me right beside him, his hand on my hip and his big body pressed to my side as we cross over to them.

"How you feeling?" Jase asks me when we reach them, regarding me critically, a frown filling the space between his eyes.

"Hungover," I say with a small, embarrassed smile. "But I'm okay, steadier now, just a headache."

He lets out a humorless laugh. "Five stitches isn't okay. They clear you for a concussion?"

I shake my head gingerly, the motion sending shards of pain shooting through my skull. "Um … no," I say. "The doctor said I should sleep, but someone needs to wake me every couple hours to make sure I wake up easily."

I feel Vance suddenly stiffen beside me, his muscles cranking tight. "Let's get her home," he says, slipping his arm from my waist, and opening the back door on Jase's black sedan. He looks at me, his dark eyes stormy. "Get in, Piper."

I eyeball him for a moment, wondering what the hell has gotten into him. He's been a moody, broody mess since the ambulance arrived and carted me off. Everything about his rigid muscles and the ticking of his jaw screams that he's pissed off. Whether it's at me, or at the fact that I have a concussion, I don't have a clue.

"Um …" I start, and then stall, considering my options. "I should probably go to Kim's."

Wes lifts a brow, his expression stern. "You think that's smart?"

I shrug, not really sure why it wouldn't be. "She'll wake me up."

He smirks, shaking his head. "She was out cold by the time I got her home. Had to carry her up to bed, and Jimmy wasn't much better off."

"You're going home," Vance says, his tone non-negotiable. When I don't move, he leans in to my side once more, his hand sliding to my lower back, and his thumb stroking my skin through my thin shirt. "I'll stick around tonight. Make sure you're okay."

I frown at Vance, and he gives me a look that tells me he's not going to listen to a single protest.

When he gestures for me to get in, I oblige, climbing into the back seat. I know there's no point in arguing and the truth is, I'm somewhat glad he wants to stick around.

Okay, wait. I'm really glad. Ecstatic, actually.

The ride back to my house is tense and ... awkward. I want to jump out of my own skin. I don't know what to say, or what to make of Vance's uptightness, and he isn't giving me any indication of what made him so unhappy.

And as for Jase and Wes ... well, they're no better, both looking just as broody as Vance.

By the time we make it to my house, my head is beginning to throb and the blood in my hair has started to dry, turning crusty. A shower is in order before the freezing around my stitches wears off.

We make our way inside, and Vance disables the alarm. I don't bother to ask why Jase and Wes are coming along, because I figure if the car ride is any indication, I won't get much of an answer.

"I'm going to shower before the freezing wears off," I say, kicking off my shoes. "Is there anything I can get you guys before I go?"

Vance stares at me for a moment, and for the first time since the ambulance showed up, amusement touches his lips. "I'm here to look after you," he says. "Not the other way around."

"Right," I say with a little nod. "Um, okay, but if you need anything ... just make yourself at home, okay?"

He smiles. "Sure, Piper. Go on and shower."

I make my way through the house, turning on lights as I head to my bedroom, gathering up a change of clothes, before locking myself in the bathroom and turning on the water.

I shimmy out of my jeans, taking my panties with them, and struggle to get my top off without catching my hair. I don't bother throwing the clothes in the hamper, just leave them where they fall, and climb into the shower, letting the hot water wash over me.

I stand under the spray for a few minutes as the hot water warms my skin and eases my taut muscles, before I grab the shampoo and get to work, carefully massaging it in around the stitches, and rinsing out the blood.

It takes three washes before I'm confident that my hair is clean. I quickly scour the rest of my body before turning off the water and stepping out, smelling of coconut.

I scour my dresser and closet for something to put on, and end up settling on a pair of gray yoga pants and an oversized tee, figuring that since Vance has already witnessed me vomiting tonight, what I wear now isn't going to make a difference, so I might as well be comfortable. I scrub my teeth, carefully comb the knots out of my hair, and then scamper out of the bathroom to find Vance.

I stroll down the hall, arms crossed over my chest as I seek him out, wondering if Jase and Wes are still around. I head to the living room, and I hear Wes's voice as I approach the doorway.

"Not your fault, man," he says. "And I'm really not seeing where exactly it is you think you failed her tonight. The tire came off and as far as I can see, you did everything you could to keep her from getting hurt. If you didn't hold her in her seat like you did, this shit could've been a hell of a lot more serious. So pull it together, and help us figure out where we're supposed to go from here."

What? Vance thinks this was his fault? He thinks he failed me?

My mind can't even begin to process this.

I stall a few feet from the door, not wanting to interrupt. I know I should just walk in and let them know I'm here, but I just stand in place.

Call it curiosity.

Call it nosey.

Whatever.

"Shit, okay," Vance says after a moment, blowing out a long, noisy breath. "You're right."

"Thank fuck," Jase says. "So are we all on the same page that tires don't just fly off vehicles and that someone most likely tampered with her truck?"

I shiver. I'm not sure if it's my hangover or head injury or their words that cause it.

"Yeah," Vance says. "We gotta get a hold of Sam; see if we can get our hands on the security video he has for tonight. He's got a couple cameras in the parking lot, maybe it picked something up we can use."

There's more silence for a moment and my heart is pounding so hard that I'm certain they can hear it, that they know I'm standing here, listening.

The silence stretches.

It's deafening.

I consider turning around, not sure I want to hear all their suspicions and plans, but my legs seem to have another idea. Before I fully register what I'm doing, I'm standing beside the couch where Vance is sitting, elbows on his knees and hands dangling between spread legs.

"You guys think someone loosened my tire?" I ask. "Who the hell does something like that?"

"My guess," Wes says, reclining back in his chair, "it's the same person who's been screwing around here."

I gape at him. "Really?"

Jase nods, crossing a leg over his knee. "If we're right that it wasn't just an accident, then yeah, it makes the most sense it's the same person."

I shiver again, though this time I'm certain it's from the topic and not simply because I'm cold or hungover or my head is throbbing.

Vance sees it, and his eyes soften. "You should go to bed."

"Vance," I say, hating that my voice trembles over his name, "do you agree with them?"

His lips press into a thin line, but his eyes stay soft and concerned. "We don't know anything for sure, Piper. This is all just speculation. Nothing for you to worry about, so go on and get some sleep, yeah?"

"No," I say immediately, shaking my head. My insides are nearly vibrating with the need to know why Vance doesn't want me involved in this conversation. I step right over to him, dropping down beside him on the couch and folding my arms stubbornly over my chest. "Don't you dare try and put me off. I deserve to know what's going on or at least what you think is going on. I need to know."

"Jesus," he mutters, looking at me curiously. "When the hell did you get so stubborn?"

I narrow my eyes in a glare. "I've always been stubborn. You just never bothered to find out before now."

The words are out of my mouth before I can stop them, and I instantly regret them. A look of disturbance crosses Vance's face and I get the feeling that he wants to say something, refute my statement, but then Wes and Jase chuckle, and the look melts away.

"All right, guys," I snap, annoyance thick in my voice, and I pin them all with a look. "Start talking. Now."

Chapter Seven

Vance

Jase and Wes are gaping, full on, open mouth, gaping, and Jesus, but I feel my jaw starting to drop, too.

I stare at Piper. I've never seen her like this before. Never known her to be demanding, or pushy, or stubborn, and I've definitely never heard her snap.

At anyone.

Ever.

She might push a little, might make her displeasure known for a tick or two, but she's usually sweet about it, quiet about it.

I can't say I don't like this new attitude on her, because hell yes, I do. There's just something so appealing about a woman who wants something and grabs it by the balls, but it's a little after three o'clock in the morning and she looks exhausted, a little pale with thin lines around her eyes and lips that tell me she's in pain.

My chest rises and falls, air rushing in and out of my lungs, but I don't feel like I'm breathing. At the moment, I don't feel anything but an urgent need to make her feel better, and all I can think about doing is giving her the pain pills the doctor left for her and tucking her into bed.

Her glare swivels between the three of us expectantly, her hair, a deep red curtain hanging down her back, and her expression ... *Fuck*, her expression is a roiling sea of emotion. Anger. Shock. Anxiety. Concern.

She's not going to let this go.

If the tables were reversed, I wouldn't either.

Silence swallows the room, and Piper begins to fidget, wrapping the hem of her too-big tee around her finger. For the first time since she came out here, I really take her in. Baggy tee and yoga pants. She didn't bother getting dressed up for me, and I admire that. Shows me that she's grown a certain level of comfortability around me and the guys, and Jesus if that doesn't make my chest tighten and warm.

Scrubbing a hand over my face, I consider what to say. I want to tell her everything, but also nothing, because the truth is, there's really nothing to tell. Until now, she'd made it clear she didn't want me doing anything more than installing a security system, so aside from keeping an eye on her house, a chat with Kim, and the call Wes placed to Cruz, I haven't really done any poking around.

All I've got is a gut feeling to go on.

No facts.

No solid leads.

Nothing tangible to give her.

"I'm sorry," Piper blurts suddenly, her face heating with embarrassment. "I shouldn't have snapped. I'm just—"

"Don't apologize," I say, cutting her short. "Never apologize for saying something you mean."

She smiles slightly and her chest rises and falls with a heavy breath. "I know I said I didn't want you guys to look into this. I know I said it was nothing to worry about. But if you really believe that tonight wasn't just an accident, then I need your help. But I also need to be involved, so if you can't give me that, I'll hire someone who will."

I don't respond immediately, not because I don't want to, but because her blunt demands render me mute. Where the hell has this side of Piper been hiding all these years?

She regards me critically for a second ... two ... five ... before letting out a frustrated huff and turning her gaze to Jase and Wes. She lifts an eyebrow in question, urging someone to respond, but they say nothing, just sit there and watch, leaving everything up to me.

I don't know whether I love them for that, or hate them.

Sighing, I lean back, resting my head on the back of the couch. When I finally speak, my words are even and my tone, straightforward. "Wasn't planning on keeping you in the dark, Piper. Just figured with everything you've been through tonight you need sleep more than you need to know what the nonexistent plan is."

"Oh," she says, the word no more than a whispered breath, as though she's surprised, like she can't quite wrap her head around the fact that I wasn't trying to hide anything from her.

"Here's what we suspect," I continue. "You've pissed someone off enough that they felt the need to vandalize your home. If we're right, that same person kicked it up a notch tonight, going from simple vandalism to tampering with your truck, which could wind up being looked at as attempted murder. We know the cops don't have any leads, but we also know they haven't tried too hard to find any. From what our contact told us, they've been taking your complaints and adding them to the overflowing pile of break and enter and destruction of property cases they have on the go."

Piper frowns and lifts her hands to her face, rubbing the skin at her temples. "I thought there was an active investigation," she says. "The officers that came to my house told me they were looking for the person who was doing this."

I shake my head, letting out another sigh. "They may be keeping an eye out, but they haven't been actively searching for the person or for leads. Until tonight, you've been a pretty low priority, but I guarantee you that's about to change."

"You're fucking right it's gonna change," Jase grinds out. "As soon as daylight hits, I'll be pulling Cruz into this."

"Who's Cruz?" she asks, shifting her weary gaze to Jase.

"He's a detective," Jase says, giving her a reassuring smile. "A friend of sorts. We've been helping each other out on cases for a few years now."

"But if the police aren't doing anything," she says, "why do you think this detective will help?"

None of us respond immediately, none of us really wanting to broach the whys, not with everything still so fresh.

I glance at Jase, meeting his eyes as something dark and unsettled passes across their depths. I've seen that look a few times since he got back from New York, each time a little darker, a little angrier, and I don't have to guess where his mind has gone.

Officer Lawrence Peck.

The dirty cop who abused Elena, forced her into a relationship, and had her on the run for a year.

The same bastard who showed up at Jase's house trying to take her back, shot his father, and if Jase hadn't pulled the trigger, killing the man in his backyard, Peck would have taken down Cruz. As it was, one of Peck's bullets grazed Cruz's arm.

A few weeks ago I would've said we'd have to badger Cruz enough until he gave in and helped us with the case. Now, though ... now I know Cruz won't hesitate.

It's Wes who finally answers, his tone cool, almost cold, his thoughts stuck on that night. "Because, Jase saved his life."

Piper must notice the untouchable topic vibe, because she doesn't question Wes's blunt statement. She simply nods and says, "Okay. We have the detective's support. Where does that leave us in terms of trying to track this person down?"

I smile, slightly amused at her persistence and I turn to face her. "First, we get some sleep. Then, tomorrow we can start here and work our way out, canvassing the area, interviewing neighbors. See if anyone saw anything suspicious over the last couple of weeks, or maybe someone new to the area."

She hesitates, her gaze darting around the room, landing on each one of us for a second, before she nods. "Okay," she says, nodding again, although this time the motion seems to be more of an affirmation to herself than an agreement to my proposed plan of attack. "Sleep, then canvassing. I think I can handle that."

We sit there for a few minutes longer, hashing out the things

Jase is going to tackle—meeting Cruz and checking out the damage on Piper's truck—while the rest of us get some shut eye, before the guys pack it in and head out.

After walking them to the door, and giving Piper's spare truck keys to Jase, I lock the door and set the alarm. I make my way back to the living room, to find Piper, standing at the edge of the couch, arms loaded up with pillows and blankets.

She looks at me over the stack in her arms and blinks. "So, uh, my guest room is kind of my office now …"

She blushes, pink staining her freckled cheeks and nose, and her gaze drops to settle on my chest.

"Couch is just fine, freckles," I say, fighting the grin that threatens to split my lips.

Her face lightens with a smile that looks part relieved and part disappointed. "Okay, um … good," she says, setting the pile down on the arm of the couch. "Do you need anything else?"

"You mind if I take a shower?" I ask.

She nods, looking down at the blankets for a second, before turning back to me, offering a small smile. "Sure, of course. You can use the main bathroom. Let me just grab you a fresh towel."

Piper moves down the hallway gingerly, taking her time and picking her steps as though she's not entirely steady on her feet, and it twists my gut into knots as I follow her.

I want to reach out and steady her.

Scratch that. I want to scoop her up in my arms and take the burden of walking from her.

She stops at a closet across from the bathroom, opens it, and pulls out a plush burnt orange towel, handing it to me. "There's shampoo and soap under the counter," she says. "And a stash of extra toothbrushes and toothpaste, too."

An unwelcome wave of jealousy strikes me at her statement, and I cock a brow. "Why the hell do you have a stash of toothbrushes?"

She shrugs, giving me a curious look. "I'm big on oral hygiene. It's important to change your toothbrushes regularly you know."

I chuckle, fighting through the possessive urges, and remind myself that aside from her relationship with Colton, Piper never was much of a dater. No way would she keep a stash on the off chance she had a guy over.

The thought probably wouldn't even cross her mind.

Refusing to examine my reaction too closely, I take the towel and mutter, "I know, and thanks."

We stand there for a moment, staring at each other, neither of us really sure what to say or do. I want to reach out to her, pull her to me, hug her, kiss her so badly that my fingers itch and burn with need, and by the way she's looking up at me, lips parted, cheeks pinked, I really don't think she'd be opposed to any of it.

Needing to touch her, I reach out a hand, pushing a loose strand of hair behind her ear, my fingertips brushing against her cheek. She doesn't flinch, doesn't recoil from my touch. Instead, she tilts into me, her entire body veering toward me.

Cupping the nape of her neck, I lean in, pressing a kiss to her forehead. "I'm glad you're okay, freckles," I say against her skin. "Really fuckin' glad."

Her hands come to my shoulders as I start to lean back, and before I can process it, she pushes up on her tiptoes, closes her eyes, and presses her lips to mine.

I inhale a sharp breath, staggered, completely dumbfounded. *Jesus.* I don't know where it came from, but I like the bold streak that's caught hold of her tonight. Liked her standing up and demanding answers earlier, and I really fucking like her making her move now.

Her kiss is innocent and soft, almost testing. Her lips barely part as she places tiny little pecks against my mouth.

My hand tightens at the back of her neck, as my other one comes up to her hip, but I don't press her for more, letting her take the lead and only accept what she's giving me, too fuckin' ecstatic that she's giving me anything at all.

And then, the kiss changes.

Piper bends into me, pressing hard against me, her lips turning insistent. Her lips part under mine and she darts her tongue into my mouth, and I find myself fighting the urge to tangle my hands in her hair, not wanting to hurt her. Her hands curl into the collar of my shirt, and my pulse kicks up and so does my cock.

Jesus, she feels so good pressed against me, tastes so good, mint mixed with a sweetness that's entirely hers. *So right.* Like this is where she's supposed to be.

Shit. I'm supposed to be here to look after her, supposed to make sure she rests, and here she is getting me so worked up that if I don't stop now, she won't be getting any rest.

With another swipe of my tongue along hers, savoring her taste, I force myself to pull back.

I don't want to.

Fuck, I really don't want to, but I do.

She's panting, her eyes glassy from lust or pain, I'm not entirely sure. It almost looks like both. They flick up to mine for a tick, before falling back to my mouth and I nearly groan as her pretty little pink tongue darts out, licking along the seam of her lips.

"Wow," she says. "We should have done that years ago."

A startled laugh slips from my lips. "Yeah, we should have."

I stare at her and she stares right back at me.

In that moment, I can't remember what I'd been waiting for all these years, why I hadn't made a move for her. All my reasoning, all my hesitations seem stupid, a waste.

Five, ten, fifteen seconds pass.

Her cheeks flush. The soft pink is so damn pretty on her skin.

"I should …" she starts, and then stalls, taking a step back. "… Um, let you have that shower."

She stares at me again, this time almost … expectantly. She wants to stay. I can see it burning brightly in her forest green eyes.

"Yeah," I say, surprising myself with my agreement and I force myself to turn away, with the fresh towel in hand. I'm halfway in the bathroom when she places a hand on my arm, drawing me to a stop. It's a barely there touch, but I feel it through my entire body. Her hand is soft, manicured, and smooth; nothing like my rough and calloused ones. I breathe out a long sigh and turn to look at her, leaning back slightly because she's staring up at me with sad forest green eyes, her expression suddenly … broken.

My gut clenches. I'm going to strangle whoever it is that's responsible for putting that look there.

"Vance …" she trails off, and all I want to do is scoop her up, take her to bed, climb in there with her, and make her feel better. Make her feel good.

My cock jerks at the thought, completely onboard with the idea.

Shit. Totally inappropriate.

She's hurt.

She's scared.

She's been through hell tonight.

The last thing she needs right now is me mauling her.

"Go get some sleep," I say, my voice coming out harsher than I intend it to. "I'll wake you up in a couple hours."

She opens her mouth to argue, or perhaps it's to say thank you, but she doesn't get the chance to do either, because I slip out of her hold, shut the door and turn on the shower, letting out a breath I hadn't even been aware I was holding.

I take a long second to collect myself, reminding myself of all the reasons why it's a bad idea to follow her to her bedroom right now, before stripping down and unwrapping the tensor bandage from my wrist.

I jump under the water; the burn from the too hot temperature is a welcome distraction. For good measure, I flex my fingers, groaning at the stab of pain that shoots through my wrist, but it does little to help.

My mind stays fixed on Piper.

My hand remembering the feel of her hip in my grasp, my lips dying for another taste.

The woman is perfection.

Shit. She always was.

I groan again, snagging up the shampoo and squirting out a

blob of coconut scented soap. I take my time, washing out the remaining dirt and slivers of glass from my hair, forcing myself not to think about how she's just a couple of doors down, curled up in bed.

When I finish, I dry off, put on my boxers, and rewrap my wrist, before heading straight for the couch, purposefully not glancing toward her room.

I lay there in the dark for a long moment, my pulse still thrumming hard, and before I close my eyes, I set the alarm clock on my phone to wake Piper in two hours.

Chapter Eight

Piper

Something startles me awake.

I sit straight up in bed, disoriented, my head pounding and my heart hammering in my chest. The room is semi dark, the lights off and blinds drawn with only thin strips of light coming into the room from around them.

A glance around tells me that I'm alone and a glance at the clock tells me that it's two o'clock, and judging by the light streaming in from the window, that would be two o'clock in the afternoon.

Sighing and rubbing my eyes, not sure what woke me up, I stand, stumbling out of bed. As my feet hit the ground, my head spins, my mouth waters, and my stomach flip-flops.

Oh crap.

Oh crap.

Oh crap.

Not again.

Hand flying up to my mouth, I half run, half stagger to the bathroom, my stomach heaving and bile rising, burning up my throat. I drop to my knees, hovering over the toilet, and retch for the sixth time since the accident.

With nothing left in my stomach, the dry-heaves feel as though they last for hours, twisting my gut, making my eyes water and my head throb painfully.

But then they end.

Thank God they end.

Leaning back on my haunches, I flush the toilet, and then sit there for a long moment, trying to catch my breath, before finally rolling up to my feet and moving over to the sink to brush my teeth, groaning when I catch sight of myself in the mirror.

I look like death.

My eyes are bloodshot and watery, my cheeks puffy, and there's the beginnings of a purplish bruise forming along my hairline and seeping in to my right cheek. My hair is a tangled mess, knotted and dented from falling asleep with it still wet, and my tee, dampened with sweat around the neckline.

Ugh. How many times did Vance see me like this last night? He woke me up … four times? Five?

Great. Too many.

Grimacing, I try to fix myself up, running my fingers through my hair, not quite brave enough to use the hairbrush. The skin around the stitches feels as though it's burning, my scalp feeling too tight from the pull of them.

My efforts do little to help, and giving up, I grab an elastic and tie my hair back loosely at the nape of my neck, before splashing some water on my face.

As I'm brushing my teeth, I hear the door to my room open and the light sound of footsteps on the floor.

Vance.

I guess another two hours has gone by already. I just hope he hasn't brought another plate of food with him this time. I don't think my stomach can handle it.

Rinsing my mouth and toothbrush, I turn off the faucet and step back into my bedroom, blinking my eyes against the bright light that's now streaming in through the open blinds.

When my eyes focus, they land on Vance leaning against the window frame, arms folded over his thickly muscled chest. My footsteps falter, and I pause, only a few steps out of the bathroom. He meets my eyes, his brown ones dark, stormy with concern.

Instinctively, I fold my arms over my chest in a futile attempt to shield the state of my sweat dampened shirt, and my overall gross appearance.

The action makes him frown, but he doesn't say anything. He only stares, his eyes carefully blank, as they scan me over.

I'm not sure what I should say, or what to do, or how I should even feel. I nearly puked on him last night, snapped at him, kissed him, and then had him hold my hair while I puked some more.

My cheeks heat with embarrassment. I want to apologize. I want to thank him. I want to run back into the bathroom and lock the door.

This is so awkward.

I just stare back at him, fighting the urge to fidget.

After a moment, his frown lines soften ever so slightly. "You're awake."

"Yeah, just barely."

Ugh. My voice sounds rough, scratchy and hoarse, and my throat feels like sandpaper.

"You get sick again?" he asks.

A lie springs to the tip of my tongue, but I quickly swallow it back, knowing he'll probably want me to eat if I say no. "Yeah."

He nods, eyeing me critically. He looks well rested and wide awake, and I'm not sure how he's pulling it off. Even if he hadn't crashed on my couch, which couldn't have been all that comfortable, he was up every two hours with me, waking me up and holding my hair while I puked my guts out.

"How's the head?" He raises his eyes questioningly. "Headache still there?"

"Better." A lot better than when he saw me last. "The headache's almost gone, nowhere near as bad as the last time you woke me."

Vance's expression shifts, and he stares at me, his eyes narrowing. He doesn't say a word, but he doesn't need to. I can tell he doesn't believe me.

"Really, it's fine," I say quickly. "The skin is sore and tight and throbbing a little around the stitches, but the headache isn't as all-consuming as it was."

He considers me for a moment, looking nowhere near as impressed by this as I am. He sighs. "I gotta run out for a bit. Kim's coming over to stay with you."

My stomach sinks. "You're leaving?"

"Yeah. I just talked to Sam and he agreed to let me review the security tapes from last night. He's meeting me at the pub in forty-five minutes. The detective I told you about last night is gonna be there, too."

I frown, hugging myself tighter, my gaze holding his. "I want to go with you."

He shakes his head, pushing off the window frame to stroll through my room, back toward the door. "Not this time. Not until you can hold down some food for more than ten minutes."

"It's just a hangover," I say, darting in front of him and blocking the doorway, before he can leave. "It'll pass."

"I hope you're right, freckles," he says. "But you're still not coming with me."

He stares at me, his eyebrow cocked, as though he's waiting for me to protest, and once again, I find myself at a loss for something to say. I know he's right. I should stay home, get some more sleep, eat, but I feel like I'm losing a battle here. My control over my life, over my stalker situation, is slipping from my grasp, and it terrifies me.

I need to be involved.

I need to be doing something.

I need to be in control.

Reaching out a hand, he runs his knuckles along my cheekbones. "But if your stomach doesn't settle soon," he says, "then I'm taking you back to the hospital. Repeated vomiting isn't normal after a concussion."

My chest squeezes, and I lean into his touch. The sudden urge to let him soothe and take care of me is nearly overwhelming. I know that he will if I just fully let go of everything and hand it over to him, but I can't just sit back and wait for the next attack.

It's just not me.

"I'm fine," I say softly. "Thank you for trying to take care of me, Vance."

He shoots me a sardonic smile and drops his hand from my cheek. "Trying. So far my success rate seems to be fifty/fifty though."

I stall at those words. "How do you figure that?"

He lifts his bulky shoulders in a shrug. "Managed to get the security system in, but you still ended up in the hospital under my watch."

"It's because you were there, because you held me in my seat, that all I got was a few stitches and a headache. In my books, that's a complete success."

He regards me peculiarly for a moment, and it looks as though he's about to say something, just as the alarm starts to beep, and we both shift our gazes to the monitor, perched on top of my dresser, reading the warning flashing there. *Front door motion detected.*

Kim, most likely.

Sighing, I pad over to the monitor, tapping the screen and quickly pulling up the front door feed, just as the doorbell rings.

Wincing at the sharp bursts of sound, I squint at the screen, and sure enough, it's Kim and Jimmy.

Vance caught my wince. I know it the moment I turn back to him. His eyes darken, his frown tightens, and his eyebrows dip low. "You need to go back to the doctor."

"I'm fine," I say, waving a dismissive hand. "Noise sensitivity directly correlates with hangovers and headaches."

His frown deepens further. "You said your headache was better."

I roll my eyes. "I said it was almost gone and not as bad as the last time you woke me."

He merely shakes his head disapprovingly.

I look away from him then, moving over to the closet, searching out a clean shirt. "You mind getting that?" I ask, pulling a light blue tank off its hanger. "I need to change real quickly."

Vance says nothing as he walks away, and I watch him as he closes my bedroom door behind him.

Once he's gone, I head over to my dresser, opening the drawer and retrieving a clean bra, before shrugging out of the dirty tee and putting it on. With no time for a shower, I pull on the clean tank as I pad back over to the bathroom and quickly swipe on some deodorant.

With a sigh, I scan my pasty reflection over once more in the mirror, and knowing that there really isn't much I can do about the sickly look to my skin right now, I leave my room to find Kim and Jimmy.

Following the sounds of their voices, I walk into the kitchen and Kim's super blonde hair glints from the glare of the sun streaming through the French doors. She has on a tight pink tank and a pair of snug black denim capri pants, and by the look on her face, she's obviously still feeling the effects from last night's bender.

Jimmy is standing beside her, leaning against the kitchen counter, looking not much better for wear. He's in his signature black—black jeans, black tee—with dark circles under his eyes.

They don't notice me right away, both of them watching Vance as he scans over a piece of computer paper. "You sure this is everyone?" he asks. "No pissed off exes or old friends she screwed over?"

Kim snorts, rolling her eyes. "This is Piper we're talking about."

Unlike last night, I don't wait at the doorway, walking right in and clearing my throat, as I shoot Kim a look. "I don't have any pissed off exes, at least none that I'm aware of, and I don't make a habit of screwing over friends."

Kim turns to me, her expression showing her amusement for a second before it falls away, and her eyes widen. "Oh my God," she gasps, a hand flying up to her mouth. "Piper, you look like hell."

"Shit, Pipes," Jimmy says, his voice far darker than I've ever heard it before. His eyes scan me critically and he flicks his lip ring with the tip of his tongue. "Shit, your face is bruising up, too."

He steps over to me and tries to get a better look but I slip past him, going straight for Vance, eyeing the piece of paper in his hand, hoping like hell it isn't my list, because in hindsight, writing that thing while drinking was probably not such a stellar idea. Did I really put down Heather Tane and the coffee cup incident?

"Is that my list?" I ask, reaching out to snatch it. "I should probably redo that."

Vance shakes his head, holding the page just out of my reach. "No, this is a good start, but if we look at last night as an indication, this person is escalating and has a lot of built up anger toward you. You most likely played a significant role in their life." He cocks an eyebrow in question. "Any of these people fit into that?"

I shake my head. "No, not really."

"Don't stalkers typically try to isolate their victims?" Jimmy asks seriously. "Like make it so their victim is alone and in the end, the victim turns to them for support?"

"Not always," Vance says. "It all depends on what their end goal is." He rubs his thumb along the dip of his chin as he considers the list once again. "I'm gonna take this with me, let Cruz take a look."

"No, really," I say, really not wanting anyone else to read the asinine reasons why certain people made the list. "I should redo it first."

Vance ignores me, folding up the paper and shoving it in his pocket. I frown at him and he laughs under his breath as he leans in and places a light kiss high on my cheekbone, brushing his lips along the bruising there, before his hands come up, cradling the underside of my jaw in his palms.

He kisses me suddenly and intensely, and I gasp, caught off guard. His lips are demanding, and his tongue, persistent, licking along the seam of my lips, until I let him in.

And I do.

I let him in and I melt against him.

I want the kiss to last forever, but in no time at all it ends and he pulls away.

Still cupping my jaw, he grins. "Stay here and try to eat something, yeah? I'll call you if we find anything."

I nod jerkily as I meet his eyes. "Okay."

His lips lift with a smile and he leans back in, pressing another quick and chaste kiss on my lips, before dropping his hands and turning away without saying another word.

"Um, what was that?" Kim asks, stunned, her eyes glued to her cousin's back as he walks out the door.

I watch Vance until the front door closes behind him, before turning to her. "It was nothing," I say, with a little shrug, though the words taste like a bitter lie on my tongue. "Just a kiss."

She gapes at me, and Jimmy grins.

I roll my eyes, unable to stop myself from blushing under their stares. "Seriously, guys, it's nothing."

"That was not nothing," Kim says. "That was intense."

Tell me about it.

Jimmy eyes me peculiarly for a moment, flicking the tip of his tongue against his lip ring. "I have to agree with Kim on this one, Pipes."

I don't know what to say, or what to think. My cheeks are burning. I can feel my blush deepening and I turn to the fridge and retrieve the Brita, trying to hide it.

"What the hell happened last night?" she asks, her tone a tad irritated, as though she can't believe she has to ask the question. She gives me a torn look, as though she isn't quite sure if she wants to throttle me, hug me, or break out into a happy dance. Her expression flickers for a moment, before finally settling on curious excitement.

I grab a glass from the cupboard, filling it up, not sure how to respond to that. I should tell her about last night—that I made the first move. She's my friend—my best friend—and I know she isn't opposed to me hooking up with her cousin. The girl has been pushing me to get to know him for years now and she's always telling me that I need to be more assertive, put myself out there more.

But the words stick in my throat.

I can still feel him, taste him. Jesus, if I had have known that kissing Vance would be this ... epic, I sure as hell wouldn't have waited this long.

Okay, wait. That's not true. I have no idea where my nerve came from last night. Maybe the pain killers? Perhaps it was remnants of adrenaline from the accident? The alcohol?

I don't have a clue.

Stalling, I take a small sip of water, forcing myself to go slow just in case, even though the cool slide down my throat feels like heaven, and I glance at Jimmy for ... I don't know what. Support maybe? An easy out to this conversation?

"Don't look at me," he says, grinning. "You know she's gonna pester you until you spill."

I groan. "Okay, fine. I kissed him last night and I guess he took that as an open invitation." I lift an eyebrow, looking between them. "Anything else you need to know?"

"Uh, yeah," Kim says seriously. "Where did he sleep last night?"

I laugh at that. "On the couch."

Chapter Nine

Vance

It's a little after two thirty in the afternoon when I arrive at Constant Pub.

The parking lot is nearly empty. There's only an unmarked cop car sitting cock-eyed across two parking spaces, with Detective Jacob Cruz leaning against it, a file folder in one hand, and the other dug into his short brown hair.

Jase and Wes aren't here yet, though I'm not really surprised. I'm almost fifteen minutes early, and knowing them, they'll be here with five minutes to spare.

I pull up close to Cruz, swinging my truck into a space a few over from his jacked-up parking job. I don't dawdle cutting the engine and getting out, anxious to see if he has any insight on Piper's situation.

Cruz looks up at me as I approach, lifting his square jaw in greeting. "About time one of you showed up."

"What are you talking about?" I ask him, raising an eyebrow. "Meeting's at two forty-five."

"You've got to be shitting me," he replies, his voice a low growl. "I'm gonna kill Jase. I thought we were past this shit."

He's dead serious as he says it, and I let out a laugh, shaking my head. About a year ago, Cruz showed up to a meeting five minutes late. It was a joint case we were working on, one involving money laundering and a messy divorce. Long story short, Cruz was supposed to arrest the husband on money laundering charges, and almost lost his shot because of those five minutes.

"What time did he tell you?" I ask, grinning wide. I swear each time Jase adds a few more minutes just to piss Cruz off.

"Two fifteen," he says, closing the file and tossing it onto the hood of the car. "Thirty minutes is a bit excessive, even for him."

I shrug, smirking at him. "You know Jase has a thing about being punctual."

"Five goddamn minutes late one time ..." He grumbles, and then stalls, his voice trailing off as he shakes his head and lets out a deep sigh, fixing his eyes squarely on my face. "You look like shit."

"I feel like shit," I mutter under my breath, leaning against his car, shifting uncomfortably. My entire body aches; the skin covering my ribs on my left-hand side is bruised and tight, and every muscle, every tendon in my right arm feels as though it's torn and stretched. I'm exhausted, too. I don't think I got much more than an hour of broken sleep last night between waking Piper every two hours, and stressing the fuck out over her constant vomiting.

He frowns. "How's Piper doing?" I can tell by the look in his eyes and the slant of his mouth that he isn't asking because he should, but because he's truly worried.

I blow out a breath, low and shallow, and run my hands over my face. "I don't really know. She says the headache's fading, but she's still vomiting, claiming it's from a hangover."

He considers this for a tick, and then nods. "Could be, but if it doesn't settle down by tonight, you should take her back to the hospital."

"Told her as much this morning," I say, glancing around, my gaze settling on the file he'd discarded when I got here. "That Piper's file?"

He hesitates before turning around, picking the file back up and handing it to me. "Uh, yeah, it is. Not sure why the responding officers haven't picked up on this and acted, but I'm pretty confident that you guys are right. You're dealing with a stalker, and my guess is their motive is revenge."

I nod as I take the file. I'd already come to that conclusion myself. Opening it up, I scan over the content, finding incident reports, but nothing that I didn't already know.

"She made a suspect list," I say, setting the file back down on the hood of the car and reaching into my back pocket, retrieving the folded piece of paper. I feel my lips twitch with amusement, recalling her notes about Heather Tane and the coffee cup as I hand it to him.

Cruz studies me for a tick, before reaching out and taking it. "Typically I'd say that's good, but that look on your face isn't filling me with confidence here."

I chuckle. "Just keep in mind she was drinking when she wrote it."

He unfolds the piece of paper, studying it, his forehead wrinkling with confusion. He casts a disbelieving look my way. "Is this for real?"

"Yeah," I say, chuckling, meeting his eyes. "Piper isn't really one to make enemies. She's pretty quiet, and as long as I've known her, she's kept to herself. Not many friends, but the ones she does have are close."

Cruz stares at me.

And stares at me.

And stares at me some more.

His expression flickers between amusement and frustration, before settling into what I know as his cop face. "No pissed off exes or friends?"

I shake my head. "I asked and she said no. No one she's screwed over, no ex who might be holding a grudge. Nothing."

He brings a hand up, rubbing the back of his neck. "Jase said you've been keeping an eye on her for the last few years. You really have no idea who might be behind this?"

I let out a strained laugh. Jesus, the way he says it makes me feel like I'm the stalker. "First off, she lived with my cousin. I was keeping an eye on them both. And second, if I knew who it was, I wouldn't be pulling you or the guys into it. I would have just dealt with it."

He considers me silently for a second, still rubbing his neck before dropping his hand, and I can practically see the cop wheels turning behind his eyes. He picks up the folder, and pulls a pen out of his pocket, jotting down a few notes on the outside as he asks, "Have you looked into her family? Could be that the stalker is trying to get to her to punish them, not her."

"It's possible, I guess."

"Dig into them and get her working on another list," he says. "If you give me the names and locations of her family, I'll run checks on my end, too, and see if anything turns up."

"I appreciate it, Cruz."

I rattle off the names of her family members and some identifying information, ages, where they live. I give him as much as I can remember off the top of my head. Cruz scribbles it down on the outside of the file folder, making notes of everything and adding a few questions of his own.

As we're finishing up, my phone beeps, and I dig it out of my pocket, checking the display. *Piper's house. Front door motion detected.*

My stomach sinks and my insides coil as I tap the screen, unlocking the phone and accessing the security system app. I know Piper isn't expecting anyone, and I know no one has left the house since me. I would have gotten a notification if the doors opened or the alarm was reset.

Waiting impatiently for the front door feed to load, I consider getting a new phone, or maybe changing my service provider, because it really shouldn't take this damn long to pull up the feed.

"Everything okay?" Cruz asks from beside me, his tone tight with concern.

I cut him a sideways look. "Someone's at Piper's house and this goddamn feed is taking forever to load."

His eyes fly wide open. "You're monitoring her house?"

"Yep." I don't know why he's surprised at that. Jase told him about the system we put in. What's the point of having a system if it isn't monitored?

Glancing back down at my phone, I squint at the image as the feed begins to take form, and frown at what I see there. "It's a courier service. One of those small same day ones."

Cruz sighs. "She runs a business from her house. It's probably something to do with that."

"Could be," I say, watching as the guy rings the doorbell and a couple seconds later the door opens and Jimmy appears. He smiles at the courier, signs the clipboard, and accepts the package before closing the door.

It all looks innocent. Just a regular delivery.

The courier doesn't hang around, turning away, and moments later, he's back in his van and pulling out of the driveway.

Sighing, I stare at the screen for a second before closing the app and stuffing my phone back in my pocket, feeling my chest loosen slightly, though the urge to call her and be sure everything's okay winds through my gut.

I'm about to pull out my phone again and make the call when Cruz pushes off the car and says, "Look who finally decided to show up."

Piper

The outside motion sensors start to beep and I wince at the sound. My head is pounding so badly it feels as though my brain is trying to fight its way out, thrashing against my skull. After the beer I had here last night, mixed with more beer and shots at the pub, and the nasty gash on the side of my head, I'm not entirely surprised, but I really, really wish it would stop.

Groaning, I let my head fall to the table top, relishing the feel of the cool wood against my heated forehead. First thing I'm doing when this is over is having all those sensors pulled out. Seriously, motion sensors for outside are the stupidest invention ever.

So damn loud.

"Somebody make it stop," I whine, rolling my head back and forth against the table. "Please."

Pushing his chair back, Jimmy stands up. "I'm on it," he says, just as the doorbell rings in three quick shrills of sound, and I whimper.

He jogs out of the kitchen without looking back, and seconds later, I hear him punch in the code for the alarm, silencing the beeps, and then the front door opens.

"Piper," Kim hisses. I roll my head to the side, glancing up at her noting her weary expression. "He's avoiding. I'm worried."

I blink at her, drawing a blank. I have a headache and I feel like I'm going to hurl again. I just can't drudge up the effort to figure out what she's talking about.

"What?" I ask, swallowing hard, trying to ignore the queasiness. Oh God. I probably shouldn't have scarfed down that huge plate of eggs and bacon and toast, but the water stayed down, and so did the coffee, and my stomach was grumbling for food.

"Tara," she whispers. "She's pregnant."

"What?" I ask again, the high pitch in my voice hurting my head even more. I pull myself up, sitting up straight in my chair, gaping at her.

"That's what the words were about last night at the pub. He told me when we got back to my place." She makes a face at me, somewhere in between annoyance and pity, twisting her napkin in her hands. "I know you're feeling like shit right now, but you need to talk to him. I've been trying, but he won't listen to me."

Closing my eyes, I try to think.

"She's pregnant?" I ask, swallowing again, and Kim nods. "And he just ... ran out of there when she told him?" I shake my head, not quite believing it. "Holy crap."

"Kim, mind your own goddamn business," Jimmy says, his voice cutting through the room like a serrated blade. "Piper doesn't need to hear about this shit right now."

"I think I do," I say, turning toward Jimmy.

He doesn't respond, but his icy eyes cut from Kim to me, his face heating with anger. He holds my stare for a long moment, his nostrils flaring, and his lips pulled tight. If I didn't know him as well as I do, I'd be freaking out right now. As it is, I'm having a hard time not squirming under his glare.

Finally he says something.

"You got a package."

"Jimmy," I say softly, but stall, when his eyes flare again.

I exchange a quick look with Kim, and she shrugs helplessly. Lots of help she is.

Pulling my bottom lip between my teeth, I glance back at Jimmy, meeting his angry eyes. Something isn't right here. This isn't like Jimmy. Not at all. He's one of the most dependable people I know. He's a good man, has a good heart. He wouldn't just walk out.

He wouldn't.

For an instant I consider pushing the topic, but the truth is, I'm just not feeling up to it, and clearly, he isn't either. "I get it. You don't want to talk about it now, that's fine, but we're going to talk about it." Then, looking to shift the subject to something less hostile, I lift my chin. "What's in the envelope?"

Jimmy doesn't respond, instead, tearing into the envelope, reaching in and pulling out a single sheet of paper. He stares at it for a second.

Five ... ten ... fifteen ...

His eyebrows dip, his face flushes red, and he mutters, "Shit."

"What is it?"

Silence.

Did he hear me? I open my mouth, about to ask again, when Jimmy blows out a breath and I watch as he shoves whatever was in the envelope back in place. He looks at me from the corner of his eye, and I stiffen when I see his hand tighten seemingly involuntarily on the envelope.

"What is it, Jimmy?" I ask again.

He bites his bottom lip, fiddling with his lip ring, a sure sign that something's making him uneasy. "I think you should call Vance."

"No, he's busy with that detective," I say. "Just tell me what it is."

He hesitates, glancing at Kim and she shrugs.

"Just spit it out," she says, her eyes darting between us.

His hands clamp down even tighter on the envelope, the paper crinkling in his grip. "It's ..." he starts, and then stalls, letting out a hesitant breath. "It's a photo of you throwing up on the side of the road with Vance holding your hair back and there's a post-it note that says, 'Last warning. Stay away,' stuck to it."

"Let me see that," I say, shoving my chair back and jumping up so fast that I lose my balance, the floor suddenly going wavy under my feet. My headache flares behind my eyes, and Jimmy goes blurry before me.

Swaying on my feet, I reach out blindly for the chair, needing something, anything to grasp onto.

"Whoa, you okay?" Jimmy asks, grabbing my arm, steadying me.

"Pipes," Kim calls, suddenly right in front of me, hands on my shoulders, guiding me back. "Sit back down, sweetie."

My stomach rolls and clenches. I pull in a harsh breath, shaking my head and flinching away from both of their touches, my hand flying up to my mouth, and I bolt for the bathroom.

Chapter Ten

Vance

I'm seated at a scratched and dinged-up rectangular wooden desk with Wes, Jase, and Cruz hovering around me. My elbows rest on the tabletop, my chin in my hands, and I'm watching the split screen of feeds from the parking lot last night.

After showing us where the digital feed dumps its video footage on the computer, Sam took off out front to stock the bar, leaving us to do our thing. It didn't take long to cue up the feed to the moment Piper's truck pulled into the lot and we've been watching for about ten minutes now, and so far, nothing.

"How long was she in there last night?" Cruz asks, leaning in closer, studying the feed that shows the tailgate of her truck.

"About an hour," I say. "An hour and a half max."

"This angle sucks ass," Jase grumbles. "Unless the person approached her truck from the back end, we're not gonna see shit."

He's right. The blind spot is huge. If the person was trying to hide from the camera, they could have moved in from the street, loosened the bolts, and left without being noticed. Except, if that were the case, it would make more sense to screw with one of the front tires, not the back. Less of a risk that way.

"There's only an hour and a half of feed," Wes says, eyes glued to the screen. "We might get lucky."

My cell phone buzzes with an incoming text message, distracting me from the conversation, and I pull it out of my pocket, glancing at the screen. It's a message from Kim.

> Kim: When are you coming back?

> Me: Just got started here so probably an hour, maybe two. What's up?

> Kim: Piper got a package. Sending you some pics now.

I lean forward, pausing the video playback, my eyes shifting from my phone to Cruz. He frowns at me. "What's going on?"

"Kim's sending me pictures of whatever was in that package," I say.

Wes narrows his eyes at me. "What package?" His tone is harsh, clearly unhappy that he's only hearing about it now.

"Same day courier showed up at her house just before you guys got here," I respond. "Jimmy answered the door, signed for it, and the courier left."

Wes nods, and his expression softens, seemingly content with my response. He should be. He knows that if I'd thought there was something *off* about the transaction, I wouldn't be here now.

My phone starts buzzing again and I quickly tap on it, bringing up the first image. It's a note, sloppily handwritten, on what looks like a lime-green post-it note, and I have to enlarge it to make out the words. *Last warning. Stay away.*

Frowning, I pull up the next image and my stomach roils. *Sonofabitch.* It's a shot of Piper and me from last night just after the accident.

"The stalker was watching last night," I say, my voice a low snarl, my hand clenching tightly around the phone. "He was fuckin' watching and taking goddamn pictures while she puked on the side of the road."

"Send them," Jase says, already digging his phone out of his pocket.

I thumb my screen, sending the images in a group text to the three of them. Phones chime and buzz, and a second later a stream of curses fills the room as the guys study the photos.

I tap out another message to Kim.

Me: She okay?

Her response is immediate.

Kim: I don't know. She's locked herself in the bathroom. It sounds like she's getting sick again.

Me: On my way.

Standing up quickly, I grimace at the stabs of pain that shoot through my body. "I'm heading back to Piper's," I say. "She's locked herself in the bathroom."

"I'll follow you," Cruz says. "I want to get my hands on that package. We might be able to get some prints off the photo or note."

Glancing at Jase and Wes, I ask, "You two mind sticking here and finish up watching the feeds?"

Jase nods, and Wes rolls his eyes as though to say, *of course.*

"Sure," Wes says. "We'll finish it up."

The drive from Piper's house to Constant Pub took me fourteen minutes. To get back, it takes me eight. I park my car in the driveway, and I'm already halfway to the door, keys in hand before Cruz even pulls in.

The alarm is off and the door is unlocked when I make it there. Jimmy didn't bother to reset it and lock up after the courier. I push against it, shoving it open, not bothering to close it with Cruz only a few seconds behind me.

I hear footsteps coming down the hall as I move toward it.

"Vance, is that you?" Kim calls, her voice sounding rattled. I don't have a chance to respond, before she appears in front of me, Jimmy on her heels. "I didn't hear the alarm."

"That's because Jimmy didn't reset it," I grind out, glaring at him over her head. "He didn't lock the door either." The guy has enough sense to look ashamed by the slip up.

"Shit," he says, as he looks around, looking at everything except for me now. "Sorry."

I shake my head, gritting my teeth against a swell of annoyance. "Where is she?"

"She's still in the bathroom," Jimmy says. "She won't open the door."

Before I can even respond to that, Kim's grabbing a hold of me, towing me down the hallway toward the main bathroom.

"Can you pick the lock or something?" she asks, a slight tremor in her voice. "She's talking, but …"

"Kim," I say, cutting her off, but keeping my tone as gentle as possible. She's stressing, on the verge of all-out panic, and that's the last thing Piper needs right now. "Jake Cruz was right behind me. Why don't you go on out there and meet him. Give him the package, yeah?"

She looks at me with shock. "But Piper …"

"She's gonna be fine," I say firmly. "Go on and meet Cruz."

She hesitates, silence consuming the hall for a second, before she finally nods and slowly turns away.

"What can I do?" Jimmy asks.

My response is immediate. "Go get her a glass of water. She's gonna need it."

He heads to the kitchen without a word, his footsteps hurried, and as he goes, I turn to the bathroom door, lift my hand, and knock.

Piper

"Go away," I growl, cracking my eyes open and glaring at the door.

I swear between Jimmy and Kim, my headache is never

going to break. Their constant knocking, constant worried shouts and questions are only making the pounding in my head worse.

I'm lying on my back on the floor—the cool tiles are a welcome relief against my heated skin—with a damp, now lukewarm, cloth on my forehead.

I'm about to close my eyes, when the thumping on the door comes again, louder this time, more demanding, and my eyes snap wide open. "Open the door, freckles."

Vance.

I close my eyes at the sound of his voice, cringing. He sounds worried and pissed off. Really pissed off.

Sighing, I drag myself off the floor, using the toilet seat and towel rod for support, and trudge across the room, moving far slower than I want to.

It takes a few seconds of fiddling with the lock, turning the little button in the knob this way and that, before I finally manage to get the door open.

Vance stands on the other side in the hallway, his expression drawn tight with concern. He doesn't say anything right away, his gaze raking over me, taking me in from head-to-toe, before blowing out a long breath. "Piper ..."

"I told them not to call you," I say, my voice coming out small. I sound like I've been eating glass, my throat raw. "I know you have better places to be, more important things to be doing than babysitting me."

"You're sick," he says incredulously, his dark eyes piercing into me. "Really sick. This is exactly where I should be."

I look at him with disbelief. I don't have a clue how to respond to that. I feel too awful, too tired, to even process it.

"Come on," he says, moving in close and wrapping an arm around my waist. "Let's get you changed and back to the hospital."

I don't protest. I don't think I could even if I wanted to. I'm drained. Completely and utterly wiped out. And the truth is, I don't know what's wrong with me.

Hangovers don't last this long.

A mild concussion wouldn't cause these effects.

The hospital is exactly where I should be.

My vision blurs and my body burns as I shuffle down the hall toward my room, using Vance for support. He helps me over to the bed, leaving me there as he goes to my closet, pulling a clean tank off a hanger, and black yoga pants from the shelf, and hands them to me, before stepping out, giving me privacy to change.

Gripping the bedframe to steady myself, I struggle to get my clothes off, and the new ones on, letting out a stream of silent curses before I finish.

Vance is standing at the door when I emerge, a glass of water in his hand. "You wanna try to drink something?" he asks, offering it to me.

I shake my head, wincing at the movement. "That's probably not a good idea."

He frowns at me, but he doesn't push it, wrapping his free arm around me, and helping me down the hallway.

Kim and Jimmy are standing in the living room, hovering. They both look anxious, and I try to placid them with a reassuring smile, but I don't really think I pull it off.

There's a man with them that I don't know, standing back a little, closer to the door. He's tall, about the same height as Vance, with dark brown hair and dark brown eyes, dressed in jeans, a sea-green tee, and there is a badge and gun clipped to his belt at his right hip.

He brought the detective with him?

"You ready to go?" the man asks in a deep voice, his eyes scanning me over, much in the same way Vance's had.

"Yeah," Vance says, handing the water off to Jimmy, and taking my purse from Kim. He reminds them to lock up and set the alarm when they leave, not giving either of them a chance to do anything but nod, before he's hustling me out of the house and helping me into an unmarked police car.

The drive to the hospital is not fun. I lay across the backseat of the cop car, my head in Vance's lap. All I want to do is close my burning eyes, just rest them for a second or two, but I swear, each time they drift shut, Vance feels the need to ask me another question.

He's rambling.

He's trying to keep me awake.

He doesn't believe that I'm just tired.

It isn't long before Cruz pulls to a stop in front of the emergency entrance. He exchanges a few words with Vance, something about heading to the station with the envelope and calling when we need a ride, and then Vance is helping me out of the car and taking me in.

Within minutes, I'm stashed in a little room, waiting for the doctor. Vance doesn't talk, but he stays with me, standing by my bed and holding my hand, his thumb stroking up and down along my palm.

He's stressed.

I can feel it, thick and suffocating in the air.

I try to think of something to say, anything to break the silence, but I'm drawing a blank, my brain too muddled with pain.

When the doctor finally comes in, it's a welcome distraction from the silence, until he pokes and prods at me enough I wind up threatening him with bodily harm if he asks me one more time if something hurts. I don't think he truly takes me seriously, though, because he laughs, telling me he wants a CT scan and blood work done before he leaves.

And then, silence descends once more.

My mind wanders, my thoughts going over my upcoming deadlines, wondering if I'll be able to complete the covers in time, and I consider calling Jimmy to see if he can search for potential images, or maybe even set up some quick custom shoots for them.

Then, I think about last night, about dancing at the bar and the way Vance watched me, and how he wanted the song to be played again just so I'd keep dancing. I don't think I've ever felt so pretty before. So wanted.

I let out a small laugh, the act, only managing to fuel my pain. "I can't believe I've waited three years for you to ask me to dinner and I'm missing it."

He chuckles, although it comes out strained. "Rain check?"

"Yeah," I say, smiling. "As soon as I'm out of here."

He squeezes my hand. "It's a date, freckles."

The silence comes once again, except this time, it isn't as tense, isn't as smothering. He's more at ease, standing beside me.

It's comfortable.

It's *nice*.

A few minutes later the nurse comes in, sticking me with needles and taking my blood, before wheeling me away.

Vance

Piper snores, soft, cute little sounds.

It's a little after five in the evening and I'm sitting in the visitor's chair in her room, legs stretched out, crossed at the ankles, and arms folded over my chest, watching her sleep. She looks so young, so innocent in sleep, her features relaxed and a small smile playing at her lips.

They decided to keep her overnight. The CT scan was all clear, but all the vomiting and the killer headache she's suffering from is a cause for concern, and they want to keep her under observation and get some fluids into her.

I'm still not sure I understand exactly what's wrong, but from what I got, it sounds like a mix of everything, the perfect storm. Mild concussion, hangover, and stress causing her to vomit, leading into dehydration, which caused the severe headache, dizziness, and more vomiting.

They hooked her up to an IV, the line running from her right arm and leading to a machine that's pumping a clear liquid into her, and they gave her a shot for the pain, which promptly knocked her out about thirty minutes ago.

Before she passed out, she made me promise to stay with her, saying she didn't want to be here alone.

I agreed. Of course I agreed. There's nowhere else I'd rather be, and the smile that lit up her face when I promised her I'd be right here when she woke up was fucking phenomenal, like I was giving her the best goddamn gift she could get.

Sighing, I drag my eyes away from her and pull out my phone. I fire off a bunch of text messages, letting everyone know she's okay and that we'll be staying here for the night. I get a bunch of messages back almost immediately, all with a similar *glad she's okay* response.

I read them all, then delete them, before putting my phone away and leaning back in the chair, shifting around, trying to get comfortable, but it's hard. My muscles ache; I'm stiff and sore from last night.

I'm considering getting up and finding a nurse—maybe I can get a mild pain killer or muscle relaxant or something—when my phone buzzes in my pocket with a new message. I fish it out, tapping on the screen, and pull up the message.

Jase: We found something.

Chapter Eleven

Vance

"It's ..." I stall, searching the image clasped in my hands. "An arm with a crappy tattoo." I glance at Jase and Wes, lifting a questioning brow, as we stand in the hallway at the hospital, just outside Piper's room.

"No," Wes says and pauses, theatrically leaning over and glancing down at the photo. "It's an arm holding a tire iron, sporting a very descriptive tattoo."

Descriptive? I laugh once, looking at him incredulously. Descriptive is definitely not the word I would use.

My eyes fall back down to the blown-up print, scanning it over. The photo is slightly blurred, a still shot from the security video at Constant Pub, showing a partial arm, and a hand clasped around a tire iron, near the tailgate of Piper's truck. It's male, judging by the size and muscle definition along the forearm, and the tattoo is simple, one of those pre-made pieces picked from an album all tattoo places have.

There's nothing special about it.

Nothing overly unique or *descriptive*.

"It's a heart with some chick's name in it," I grumble.

"No," Wes declares again, this time drawing the word out, smirking at me. "It's a heart with some chick's first *and* last name in it. See ..." He snags the image from my hands, holding it up in front of me, and points, underlining each name with his finger, reading them off. "Trixie Starr. Two names. First and last."

I let my head fall forward and rub between my eyes where a headache is starting to form. When Jase said he found something, I thought it was something good, something useful. Not some fuzzy photo of a partial arm with a shitty tattoo and a few scars.

It's frustrating.

Downright maddening.

"It sounds like a stripper name," I say, glancing back up.

"Exactly." Wes wiggles his eyebrows up and down. "I'm all for tracking this chick down."

Jase groans, and I snort out a laugh.

"Who the fuck would tattoo a stripper name on their body?" I ask needlessly, knowing neither of them will have an answer.

Wes shrugs, exchanging a look with Jase. Jase merely shakes his head.

"I sent a copy of it to Cruz before coming here," Jase says. "I know it's not much, but this shot with the tire iron is enough to get their asses in gear and seriously look into the string of vandalism she's been dealing with. He's gonna run it through the system, see if he gets any hits on the tattoo or scars."

"Doesn't mean we can't put boots to the pavement and do a little investigative work," Wes grumbles under his breath, folding his arms over his chest.

Jase cuts him a look, his eyes sharp and speculative, and Wes meets it head on with a harsh glare of his own.

Interesting.

Either Jase has had enough of this conversation, or I missed something over the last few hours.

At the moment, I'm too tired, too stiff and sore, to ask about it.

"Did Cruz say anything about that package she got?" I ask, shifting against the wall that's propping me up, straining my stiff body as I settle against it once more. Everything is aching, my arm is throbbing, my bruised up ribs are screaming for rest, and

I'm trying my damnedest to hide it.

"He's sent it to the lab," Jase says. "We should hear something by Monday at the latest."

I nod. "Let's wait him out then. See if he comes up with anything."

"Sounds good," Jase agrees, and then pauses, letting out a long breath as he looks straight at me, eyes narrowing as he takes me in. "You should go home. Get some rest."

Shit.

I guess I'm not hiding my discomfort as well as I thought.

My response is immediate, though. "Can't. Promised Piper I'd stay with her."

We all stare at each other in silence for a moment and I see the shock and subtle amusement wash into their features. Jase mutters a curse under his breath, shaking his head.

"Holy shit," Wes says. He laughs and shakes his head, too, smiling genuinely. "You're really doing this."

It's not a question, but I respond anyway. "Of course I'm doing this. I told her I'd be here when she wakes up, so that's exactly where I'm gonna be."

Jase laughs, flashing both dimples as he grins at me. "That's not what he means and you know it."

I do know, but I say nothing, letting out a resigned sigh instead.

Jase and Wes stare at me.

And stare at me.

And stare at me some more.

Their expressions are curious, their eyes boring into me inquisitively. I get the sense that neither of them are going to let this go.

"Jesus Christ," I mutter and sigh as I rub my hands down my face in frustration. "Are we really gonna have this conversation now?"

Wes shrugs. "Can't think of a better time to do it."

I can.

I can name plenty of better times than now. About a million and one better times, actually. Times that don't include me waiting around a hospital, aching and tired and miserable, for Piper to wake up.

Silence hangs between us.

I know what they're looking for, but I don't know what to say. I want to lie to them, tell them it's nothing. It would be the easiest response right now, and I like easy, but fuck, they'd see right through me.

They always do.

"Don't really know what I'm doing," I finally say. "But I'm here and I like being here."

Jase snorts out a stunned laugh and clears his throat. "You've been keeping your distance for years. What changed?"

What changed?

Everything.

Nothing.

I don't know.

I'm quiet for a moment, contemplative, as I look around the busy hallway, considering how exactly I'm supposed to respond to that. I nearly tell them it was a nasty bout of jealousy that spurred me on to finally make a move, but thankfully, my tired brain has enough sense to keep that morsel of information to myself. Jase and Wes have known Piper a long time, just as long as me, and I'm certain hearing that I jumped in without thought over something as absurd as jealousy will only piss them off.

They like Piper.

They've looked out for her in one way or another since they met her.

And I'm certain that's exactly what they're doing now.

But the thing is, I'm not really sure what I'm doing with her.

I don't know where this is going, or even exactly where I want it to go, but I do know that I sure as fuck want to find out.

I'm done holding back with her.

Done watching from the sidelines, waiting for … something to happen.

Hesitating, I straighten up, grimacing at the stab of pain that shoots through my ribs as I shove off the wall and fold my arms over my chest. "I don't have a clue what I'm doing here," I say again, shrugging my shoulders. "But whatever this is, I'm all in."

Wes laughs again, this time with a sharp edge to it, and Jase's eyes narrow as he tilts his head, shaking it slowly, his jaw clenching and twitching.

Shit.

I guess they don't like my response.

"You better figure this shit out quick," Jase says quietly, a clear warning in his tone. "She's a nice girl and she sure as fuck doesn't need you screwing things up in her life more than they already are."

I nod. *Message received.*

"Good," Wes says, his easy smile pulling his lips up. "It's about damn time you got your shit together."

I can't help but laugh, because he's right, it is about damn time, but I don't humor him with any further response. "You guys should get out of here," I say. "Nothing more we can do tonight."

Wes nods, pushing off the wall. "You need anything from your place?"

"Nope." I shake my head. "I'm good."

Jase digs a set of keys out of his pocket, tossing them to me. "Your truck's in the visitor's lot."

I catch the keys. "Thanks."

They both nod, and turn to leave, but after a step, Jase stalls, looking back over his shoulder. His jaw is firm and his eyes lock with mine for a few seconds, another warning hardening his expression, before he sighs and looks away. I shake my head, smirking, as I turn and walk back into Piper's room.

Piper

The faint scent of disinfectant hits me, making my nose twitch and itch, and sluggishly, I open my eyes.

I'm on my back in a hospital bed, my head tilted to the side with one arm wrapped around my center, and the other, tucked under my cheek. The room is quiet and dark, it's still nighttime,

I think, and there's cool air blowing down on me from somewhere above my head. I shiver, burrowing under the flimsy blanket that isn't much more than a sheet, but it does little to ward off the chill.

My head is foggy and my throat dry, after effects from all the painkillers and sleeping aids the nurses have been pumping through my veins, no doubt. I blink a few times, trying to clear the drug induced haze as I slowly roll to my side, my blurry gaze searching the room for a glass of water.

When I reach my side, my gaze lands on an unexpected sight, and I stall, my breath catching in my throat.

Vance.

He sits beside me, his dark eyes regarding me quietly. His chair is angled and pulled up close, his head beside mine, tilted toward me, and his feet are propped up on the end of my bed.

Something inside me flutters at the sight of him. There's something so ... wonderful about waking up with this man watching over me. Something so ... perfect.

I offer him a small smile, trying to get myself under control as I sit up. "You're still here."

My voice sounds hoarse and scratchy, and my throat feels raw. I swallow thickly, but it does little to help with the dryness.

He frowns, hesitating, as his eyes sweep over me. "Of course I'm still here. Why wouldn't I be?"

"I, uh ... I just thought that, well ..." I stall and clear my throat. I don't know what to say. I'm not even sure why it surprises me that he's still here. Vance isn't one to break a promise. Sighing, I drop my eyes from his, fiddling with the sheet. "I guess I just thought you'd have to leave for work or something."

Vance raises his eyebrows, a look of surprise passing across his face, as though he's shocked that I thought he'd leave, perhaps even a little hurt by it. "Told you I'd be here when you woke up, didn't I?"

My stomach begins to flutter again, so does my heart, and my cheeks heat with a flush. Ugh, I really need to get myself under control—fast.

"Well, uh, yeah, but ..." I let my words trail off, because I really don't know what to say.

He's quiet for a moment, letting his feet drop to the ground, and he turns his chair to face me. He gazes at me, his lips twitching with amusement as he takes my hand within his. "How are you feeling?"

"Better." A lot better than the last time he asked me that. "Really good, actually."

Strangely enough, I slept really well. I can't chalk it up to peace of mind, because nothing has really changed in my situation aside from the fact that I don't feel as though I'm going to throw-up anymore, but the drugs were enough to knock me out, which is a really good thing.

"Really fuckin' glad to hear that, Piper," he says, releasing a breath and smiling softly. He lets go of my hand and reaches out, brushing his knuckles along my cheek, before standing up. "I'm gonna go find a nurse," he says. "Let them know you're up."

"Wait a second," I say quickly as he turns away. "What time is it?"

He pauses, glancing down at his watch. "Ten thirty-five."

"That's it?" I ask. "I feel like I've been sleeping for days."

He stares at me for a moment, the corner of his mouth kicking up into a grin, and he chuckles. "Not quite. It's Sunday."

The moment he says it, I feel like I can't breathe, my throat closing up, my chest tightening.

It's Sunday?

Crap. Crap. Crap.

I need to get out of this bed. I need to get out of this place. Panicked, I sit up straighter and throw the blanket off, completely forgetting about the IV attached to my arm, grimacing as I nearly yank the thing out, snagging it up in the blanket.

I suck in a sharp breath. Jesus, that burns.

"Whoa," Vance says, coming right over to me and quickly untangling the blanket. "What are you doing?"

"Do you know where my clothes are?" I ask, swinging my

legs off the bed. "I'd like to go home."

"Is there a particular reason why you're in such a rush to get out of here?" he asks, a touch of humor in his voice as he clutches my hands, stilling my movement.

I stall, nodding my head slowly. "I have work to do—deadlines this week, my truck needs to be dealt with, and I'd really like to go home and make sure my house is still standing."

His brow furrows, regarding me peculiarly, as though he thinks I might be insane. "Pretty sure your clients will understand, freckles," he says calmly. "Jase had your truck moved to a body shop yesterday, and I've been watching your house. The only person who's gone in or out since you got here is Jimmy."

My eyes widen. Oh God, he's right. Blood rushes straight to my face and I feel my cheeks flame with embarrassment. I quickly look away from him, wanting to bury my face in my hands, but can't with him still holding them tightly.

Of course my clients will understand, and I already knew that Vance is watching my house. I was also there during the little meeting when Jase took my spare keys agreeing to handle my truck.

Maybe he's right to think I'm insane.

"I'm so embarrassed," I groan, closing my eyes. "You must think I've completely lost it."

"Nothing to be embarrassed about," he says, letting go of my hands and leaning forward, kissing my forehead. "Let me go find the doctor. We'll get you checked out, and then I'll take you home, or if you're hungry, we can grab a bite, yeah?"

I nod. "Okay."

He pulls away then, standing there for a moment, staring at me as though he's not quite sure if he should believe me or not, before he eventually turns away and leaves to find the doctor.

It takes a little over an hour for the doctor to make it to my room and finish checking me over. By the time he finishes poking and prodding at me, I'm hungry and grouchy, completely ready to get out of here. My stomach grumbles, begging for food, as he rattles off a long list of warnings and things to watch for, and then I'm discharged from the hospital for the second time in as many days.

We end up at a McDonalds and it surprises me, because Vance is more of a pub and draft kind of guy, but it's perfect. I don't eat fast food often, but when I do, this is the place I do it at.

Vance holds the door for me when we arrive, letting me go in first. At nearly midnight on a Sunday, the restaurant is almost empty, with only a handful of people waiting in line. As we move toward the register, lining up, he steps in close behind me, so close I can feel his breath on my skin as he places a hand on my hip, and I try really hard not to think about how awesome it feels to have this man so close.

I look over the menu needlessly. I don't come here often, but when I do, I always order the same thing: chicken nuggets with honey dipping sauce.

It doesn't take long before we're at the front of the line, placing our order, and a chicken nugget and burger meal later, we're sitting across from each other at the far end of the restaurant with our food spread out before us.

Starving, I open up the honey, soaking a nugget and taking a bite, not able to stop the sudden moan from slipping out at the taste. "So good."

Vance laughs loudly at my reaction, the sound causing me to grin. He reaches over, stealing one of my nuggets and drowning it in honey, before popping the whole thing in his mouth.

"Shit," he mumbles around the mouthful. "You're right, that is good."

I look at him incredulously. "Don't tell me you've never had the chicken nuggets here before."

"Nope," he says, shaking his head.

I raise my eyebrows in surprise. "Seriously?"

"Seriously."

"That's just ... sad," I say, dipping my nugget again and popping the rest into my mouth.

Vance shrugs and lets out another laugh, picking up his burger. "I don't typically eat this garbage."

Shaking my head, I grin across the table at him as I dig into my food. I already know he doesn't eat this stuff often, but still, everyone needs to try the chicken nugget meal at least once.

Dinner is fantastic, the food exactly what I needed to clear the remaining drug fog from my brain. I'm stuffed by the time I finish my nuggets and half my fries, and I push the rest aside, not able to eat another bite.

"Was it good?" Vance asks, watching me intently and perhaps a little uncertainly, as though he might be worried that I'm not enjoying it.

"Amazing," I say. "Best chicken nugget meal I've ever had."

He smirks, jerking his chin toward the fries. "Full?"

"Stuffed," I respond, pushing them across the table. "You can have them if you want."

He shrugs a shoulder as he nabs a fry, popping it into his mouth, eyeing me peculiarly as he chews. "So ..." he hesitates. "I've got some news for you."

My brow furrows and my stomach drops at his tone. "Good news?"

He smirks, shrugging noncommittally. "Depends how you look at it."

Ugh. That doesn't sound good.

My gaze drifts momentarily, contemplating whether or not I want to hear it, before I sigh, glancing back at him. "Okay, lay it on me."

He cocks an eyebrow as I take a sip of my cola. "You sure you wanna hear it now, because you sound pretty ... *unsure.*"

I sigh. "That's because I am unsure."

My response makes him laugh.

"I've had a really shitty couple of weeks," I explain, "and I'm having a good time. I'm just not sure I want to ruin it with *news.*"

He blinks a few times, taken aback. "Well, I wouldn't want that," he says, hesitating again before shaking his head, backtracking. "The news can wait until tomorrow."

I laugh, shaking my head. "Nope, I'm curious now. Just tell me. Let's get it over with."

He takes a sip of his drink before pushing it aside. "Okay,

then … I wanna talk about your truck and what the guys found."

I say nothing, only nodding for him to go on, trying to hide the sudden unease curling within my belly.

"Jase and Wes managed to pull a partial still shot from the security video of the guy that loosened your tire at Constant Pub."

I blink. Holy crap. It really wasn't just an accident? I know Vance never thought it was, and deep down I had a feeling he was right, but still, I wanted to believe the guys were just being paranoid. "Someone really messed with my truck."

It's not a question, but Vance responds anyway. "Yeah, freckles," he says quietly. "Someone really messed with your truck."

"Who was it?" I ask, gazing at him.

"That's where the news isn't so good," he replies. "It's only a partial image of a tattooed arm holding a tire iron near your tailgate. We don't know who it is yet, but we'll figure it out. Cruz has a copy and he's running the tat through their system. If the guy has a record, we'll get an ID through that."

"And if he doesn't?" I ask, raising a questioning eyebrow.

Vance shrugs a shoulder. "Then we find him another way."

I don't even know what to say. I reach for my cola, clutching the cup in my hands, determined not to freak out. He sounds so confident, as though finding this tiny piece of evidence is actually good news, that it will lead him to finding the jerk that's been messing with me.

And maybe it will.

Maybe this is good news.

I guess it could be if the guy has a record, and if he had the ink before he was arrested.

"Okay," I say, nodding once to myself. "Okay, this is good. It's more than we had before."

"It is," he agrees, smirking, as he leans over the table, closer to me. His gaze flicks down to my lips, holding there for a second, before meeting my eyes once more. "Now what do you say we get out of here and get you home?"

Those words, although I know they're completely innocent, send a tingle down my spine. I'm not sure if they're from nervousness or excitement. It's probably both. But hearing him say those words in that low, deep voice of his, when he's looking at me the way he is, makes my head come up with a whole lot of interesting scenarios involving us somewhere a lot less public with a whole lot less clothing.

I lean into him, seeing the pulse in his throat jump and it makes me grin. It's nice to know that he isn't immune to me either.

He kisses me then. It's quick, just a small peck on the lips, but Jesus, if that little kiss doesn't make my heart sputter and race.

I have a feeling he's going to wind up breaking my heart by the time this is over, but in the moment I don't care. In this very second in time, I'm certain any pain that comes later will be entirely worth it.

Chapter Twelve

Piper

"That's it." A cell phone flies across the room, hitting the wall so hard I'm certain it leaves a nick in the drywall. "I can't take it anymore."

I don't look up, keeping my eyes trained on the computer screen in front of me, only vaguely listening to Jimmy. I've flipped through these images at least a dozen times over the last hour, thinking that maybe if I look at them enough, one will jump out at me. I hope it happens soon, because I'm running out of time. Vance is going to be here in a little over two hours to take me to dinner, and I really need to finish this last cover before then.

Jimmy's cell phone chimes again.

And again.

And again.

He lets out a stream of curses, glaring at it from across the room, but he doesn't move to retrieve it.

Taking a deep breath, I click the next page in my search results.

Inhale, exhale.

Breathe. Relax. Focus.

There's no point in trying to talk to him. I already know what he'll say. I've heard it all repeatedly over the last few days.

She's not really pregnant ...
You don't understand ...
I don't want to talk about it ...

"She's nuts," Jimmy continues, ruining my focus once again. "Completely bat-shit crazy."

I try to ignore him, because honestly, I don't want to get in the middle of his baby drama. He's a good friend and I want to be supportive, but each time I open my mouth to say something to him, all that wants to come out is a slew of curses and nasty remarks about being a deadbeat dad. So instead of ruining our friendship, I figure it's better to pretend that he's not here and stay out of it, at least until he steps up and talks to Tara.

But ignoring him has turned out to be a useless effort.

He's been rambling on like this since he woke up and planted his butt in my office. He's supposed to be in here helping me, but so far all he's done is distract me.

I click the next page in my search results as I mutter, "Maybe you should just pick up the phone or return her text messages. I bet if you'd just acknowledge her she'd chill out."

He makes a noncommittal sound from the back of his throat, but says nothing.

His lack of response doesn't surprise me in the least. He's been shaky, and edgy, and moping around here for days, avoiding Tara, avoiding his new girlfriend, avoiding ... everything.

Shaking my head, I focus back on the computer screen. The last few days have been ... hectic. I've been alternating between hiding in my office and venturing out with Vance, working on trying to find the jerk that has been messing with me and caused our accident.

We've made progress—sort of.

We got an ID on tattoo guy.

We canvassed my neighborhood.

Each day it's something new: a new lead, a new place to check out, a new contact to confer with.

Vance is driven and apparently very much in demand. His phone rings constantly, and he's always on the run to meet a client or handle a crisis with the guys.

It never seems to stop.

Jimmy's cell phone rings and buzzes, vibrating and rattling against the floor, and he groans, long and loud. "I'm telling you, Pipes, she won't give up. It doesn't matter what I say to her. It's like she completely forgot I was there when the doctor told her there was no way she could have kids."

Those words draw my attention away from the computer. I look over my shoulder toward the lounge chair in the corner of the room where Jimmy sits, laptop on his knees. "What do you mean she can't have kids?"

He makes a face at me, one that would probably be comical if it wasn't for how clearly frustrated he is. "She had cervical cancer. The radiation therapy she had to have caused her ovaries to stop working."

Those words stall me and my stomach sinks. I gape at him. Cancer? Tara had cancer? Why don't I know this? "What? When did Tara have cancer?"

Jimmy sighs and his expression shifts, all the frustration dying away at my question. His shoulders sag, his jaw clenching as he regards me with so much pain and guilt it makes my chest ache. "About eight months ago."

"I, uh ... I didn't know." I don't know what else to say. I make a move to go to him, wanting to comfort him, needing to erase that devastating look on his face, but he lifts a hand, silently asking me to stay where I am, and I drop back into my chair.

"She didn't want anyone to know," he says and sighs. "She didn't want it to be a big thing, to have people stressing and worrying over her. Being the center of attention always freaked her out. But she's good now. They got it all with the radiation. She still has regular checkups, but that's pretty normal."

"So you, uh, it was just you helping her through it?" I ask incredulously.

"What else was I supposed to do?" he asks, arching an eyebrow in question. "It's what she wanted."

"You could've told me and Kim," I say. "Even if she didn't

want our help, we could've been there for you. My God, Jimmy, I don't ... I can't even imagine how hard it must've been on you both."

"I could have, but I didn't." He hesitates for a moment, his expression turning guarded. "Look, this is probably going to make me sound like an insensitive jerk, but we were over a long time ago. I stuck around because she begged me to, because of all the shit she was going through, but you know what, she's not my problem anymore, and her spewing these goddamn lies about being pregnant is not going to change anything between us. It's over and I'm done letting her guilt me into sticking around."

I stare at him as his words sink in. Ignoring the fact that I'm completely in shock, and that I don't know how to process all this, I feel a strange sense of relief. If what he's telling me is true, and I have no doubt it is, then he isn't turning into a deadbeat dad. He's just a guy, trying to end things with a girl who isn't ready to let him go.

"So she's not really pregnant," I say. "She's just what ... using it to try and force you to come back to her?"

He merely nods.

I eye him peculiarly, and once again, I'm at a loss for what to say. I feel a little foolish, just sitting here while one of my best friends clearly needs something, but I honestly don't have a clue what that is.

Jimmy's phone buzzes once again, and he lets out a stream of curses as he sets down his laptop and stands, thumping across my office to retrieve it. He taps the screen, bringing up the message that just came in, and swears again, this time, under his breath, before powering the phone off completely and shoving it into his pocket.

"Sorry about the wall, Pipes," he mutters, turning back to me. "I'll pick up some paint and touch it up."

I shrug. "I want to change the color in this room anyway. You just gave me the perfect excuse to do it."

He smiles at that, a real genuine smile, and lets out a light laugh. "Thank you."

I nod, suddenly not trusting my voice. I know he's saying thank you for more than just the wall. I can see the emotions brimming in his eyes, hear the sincerity, and all the meaning behind those two words in his tone.

He's saying thank you for listening.

Thank you for not judging.

Thank you for being his friend.

Silence hangs in the room as he crosses back over to the chair and takes a seat. He picks up his laptop and opens it back up, before looking back at me.

He laughs awkwardly, biting down on his lip ring. "I should probably already know this, but Vance's cop friend got an ID on the guy who loosened your tire, right?"

I hesitate, not responding right away. I don't want to burden him with my problems when he's already dealing with enough of his own, but Jimmy just sits there, eyebrows raised, regarding me patiently, if not a little pleadingly.

He doesn't want to talk about Tara anymore.

He wants a distraction.

"Yeah, he did," I say after a moment. "The guy's name is Chad Miller. He's like some career criminal or something like that. Theft, robbery, drugs. He got out of lock up like three weeks ago, right around the time all the vandalism started."

"Do you know him?" he asks curiously.

I shake my head, looking away from him, glancing around the room, not wanting him to see the sudden unease twisting me up. The whole thing is befuddling. I stared at a copy of his mug shot for hours on Monday, hoping for some kind of recognition to spark up, but I've never seen the guy before in my life.

I don't know who he is.

I don't know why he's messing with me.

It's frustrating, outright maddening.

The worst part about it is, he's still out there. Vance and the guys are looking for him, so are the police, but so far, they've come up with nothing. Not that I expected them to find him overnight or anything. It's Thursday, a little more than ninety-six hours since Detective Cruz provided Vance with the guy's ID, and tracking down someone who most likely doesn't want to be found takes time, but still ...

"Can you get a copy of his picture?"

"Um ... yeah," I say. "I've actually got it. Vance emailed his mug shot to me on Monday to see if I recognized the guy."

He grins. "Awesome. We can make some reward posters. Offer up like five hundred bucks to the person who can provide the information that leads to his location and arrest. We can post them around the neighborhood, pin them up in stores. I bet that'll help find him quicker."

I'm quiet for a moment, pondering the idea. "Do you think five hundred is enough?"

Jimmy shrugs. "I think it's enough to get some people talking. Why don't you send me the picture and I'll draft something while you work. It's easy enough to change the reward price later if you decide to."

I grin at him, feeling a peculiar sense of excitement as I turn back to my computer and bring up my email. Although Vance has let me be a part of a few things, like canvassing my neighborhood, or the briefing meetings with the guys, he's kept me out of the majority of the investigation.

Right now, he's out following up on leads to Chad's location. I tried everything I could think up this morning to convince him to let me come along today. I pleaded, I bribed, I nearly got to my knees and begged, but nothing worked, he wouldn't bend, wanting me to stay home and rest.

His worry, although completely sweet, is extremely annoying.

I'm fine. Feeling great, actually, aside from the painful pinch of the stitches in my scalp and the bruising on my cheek and ribs.

But even if Vance doesn't want me out working on the case with him, a reward ... that's something I can do to help.

I send the picture to Jimmy, considering how much to give for the reward. Aside from buying my house and paying off my student loans, which barely made a dint in my trust fund, I haven't touched the money. My design work pays the bills and gives me a little extra to have fun with, so I've just been saving it for a rainy day.

And if this isn't a rainy day, I don't know what is.

So what's a good number? Five hundred ... A thousand ... Two? Maybe I should just wait until tonight and ask Vance what amount he thinks would be enticing enough. I'm sure he's offered rewards before in his line of work; he'll know better than me.

Right, okay, just ask Vance.

Decision made, I pull up the photo stock site and get back to work, starting my search again.

An hour slips by in a blink. I actually make progress, finishing off a draft and sending it off to the author for approval. Jimmy shows me a couple of options for the flyer, and I end up settling on one that has both, a picture of Chad and a close-up of his Trixie Starr tattoo. The caption is simple, reading: Reward for information leading to discovery or arrest.

I'm just about to shut down for the day, and go take a shower, when my phone chimes. I pick it up, tapping the screen, and bring up the new text message.

Vance: Sorry, freckles, I'm gonna be late. Found Trixie Starr.

Vance

Trixie Starr is not a stripper.

The short brunette standing before me, dressed in pink floral scrubs, is so far from what I expected, it's almost laughable. She's pretty, small, and a little timid looking, and although her name hints at a career working the pole somewhere, in actuality she's a nurse and works at a retirement home in the city.

Certainly not the kind of woman I would expect to hook-up with Chad Miller, a low life druggie who's spent more time in county lock-up than out of it since he became an adult.

Trixie looks apprehensive, holding the door only partially

open with half of her tiny body shielded behind it, her eyes shifting from me, to Jase, to Wes, to our vehicles sitting at the curb at the end of her driveway.

I smile at her, hoping the gesture will put her at ease. "Ms. Starr, I'm Vance Rutherford, and these are my partners Jason Pierce and Wesley Gates. We're looking for—"

"I know what you're looking for," she says, cutting me off. Her voice is short, but soft with a subtle southern lilt. "Chad isn't around. He hasn't been home in a few days."

I stall at her abruptness, wondering just how often this woman has to put up with strange men coming to her house looking for her boyfriend.

Probably far too regularly.

She doesn't seem all that surprised that we're here, almost as though she's been expecting us. But then, I guess when you decide to play house with a man like him, you're always expecting something or someone.

Raising a questioning eyebrow, I ask, "You happen to know where we can find him?"

"That depends." She opens the door a little further, her eyes narrowed, scanning us over. "What do you want with him?"

Huh.

Perhaps I misjudged her timidness.

I consider how to respond to her question, wondering how much of the situation I should divulge. I have a feeling she's not going to be surprised to hear that her boyfriend has a warrant out for his arrest, but I can't get a solid read on how far she's willing to go to protect him.

"He's a person of interest in a case we're working on," I say after a moment. "Just hoping to ask him a few questions, is all."

She eyes me skeptically, not believing me for a second. "Are you the police?"

"No, ma'am," Wes says, shaking his head. "We're private investigators."

His words make her laugh. "Well this is new," she says and opens the door the rest of the way, stepping out onto the porch. She shakes her head, amusement flashing in her wide blue eyes.

"Private investigators."

"Not quite sure why you find that funny," Jase says, scowling down at her. "But yeah, we're private investigators, and we'd really like to find Chad before the police do."

"Sorry," she says laughing again. "It's not really funny, it's just ..." She shakes her head. "Never mind, it doesn't matter. I don't know where he is. Chad comes and goes whenever he wants. When he goes, he doesn't check in. He doesn't tell me where he's going or how long he's going to be gone. He just vanishes."

She's lying, I think, as I watch her turn away and pull the door closed, locking it. I think she knows exactly where he is, or at least she has a pretty good idea of where to start looking.

"I really wish I could help you guys," she continues, "but I can't. I have no idea where Chad is."

Jase snorts out a laugh. "I call bullshit. You know exactly where he is."

Trixie shrugs. "Believe me or don't, I really don't care, but I've got to run, so ..." her voice trails off as she turns away from us and starts for the steps.

I just stand there, watching her for a tick, not sure what to say or do. I don't know if I should tell her anything, because anything I say she could use to tip off Chad. But if I say nothing ...

Fuck.

I cut my eyes at Jase and he nods, silently agreeing that we need to lay it all out for her.

"He's been vandalizing my girl's house and freaking her out for a couple weeks now," I say quietly, and her footsteps stall immediately. "Friday night he loosened the bolts on the back tire of her truck. I was driving when it came off. The truck flipped and she wound up getting a concussion and stitches. She landed back in the hospital because of that concussion on Saturday and was kept overnight."

"Who's your girl?" she asks curiously, turning back to look at me.

I cock an eyebrow, folding my arms over my chest. "Does it

matter?"

She shakes her head. "Not really, but I'd like to know."

"Her name's Piper Owen," Jase says, before I have a chance to make up a name. "She's a sweet girl, keeps to herself. She sure as fuck doesn't deserve the bullshit your man's been dishing out."

Trixie says nothing, but her eyes widen, recognition flaring within their depths.

"You know her," Wes says. It's not a question. He caught the recognition in her gaze as well.

"No," she says quickly, backing up a step. "Sorry, but I really can't help you guys and I have to go or I'm going to be late for work."

"If you change your mind, then give me a call, yeah?" I say, fishing out my wallet and retrieving a business card, handing it to her.

She doesn't say a word, but she accepts the card before she walks away, not bothering to look back. I stand on her porch, watching as she gets in her white Honda Civic, starts it up, and pulls out of the driveway. Shaking my head, I turn back to the house, scoping it out.

"He hasn't gone anywhere," Wes says. "My guess is he'll be back at this house tonight."

"Yeah," I agree. "Guess we're in for a long night."

"Wonder how Piper's gonna feel about a stakeout instead of a steak dinner?" Jase asks, his voice full of amusement.

I groan, thinking about how much she wanted to come with me this morning, and briefly, I wonder if there's any way I can get her to stay home without flat out lying to her.

Not likely.

Chapter Thirteen

Piper

"Are you sure you don't want to come with us?" Kim shouts over the sound of my hair dryer as she comes into the bathroom. I'm bent over at the waist, blow-drying my wet hair, with a plush orange towel cinched around my chest. She hops up on the countertop across from me, her legs swinging in my line of sight. "It'll be fun."

"I'm sure it will be," I shout back, not looking up as I work the dryer over my hair. "But I think I'm just going to stick around here for a bit."

She's heading out for a drink (or ten) with Jimmy, a kick-off celebration of the start to her vacation. After my Saturday night stay in the hospital, Kim pulled some strings at work and managed to secure two weeks off. She claims it's so she can help find Chad Miller, but I'm pretty sure it's an excuse to get out of work. Her boss is an ass and he creeps her out, always hitting on her, making her uncomfortable, and she's had enough. I'm certain she's going to spend some time job hunting over the next couple of weeks, since she's already been hinting at becoming my assistant.

"If you're worried about Vance, you could—"

Before she can finish that sentence, I turn off the dryer and straighten up, looking at her. "Why would I be worried about

Vance?"

My response makes her laugh as she starts fiddling with my various body sprays and scattered hair products, lining them up along the mirror. "Because it's Vance and you've worried about him in one way or another since you first met him."

I cringe inwardly at her flippant statement, because this (unfortunately) is true, but it's more than that, too.

The truth is, this new *hanging out* thing I've been doing with Vance is driving me insane.

He pushed his way into my life, forcing me to look at him as a possibility—not just some fantasy—and I don't know what to do about it.

Half the time I don't even believe it's really happening.

More often than not, I find myself wondering what will happen when he finds Chad and life goes back to normal. Will he get bored with me? Will things just go back to how they were?

Ugh. I hate this. Hate the uncertainty. Hate the not knowing. Hate all of it.

"I'm not worried," I say, thoroughly impressed that I manage to sound semi-confident. "He said he'd be late, not that he wasn't coming."

She makes a face at me, somewhere between excitement and pity. I'm sure she's feeling both. Kim is an all-out advocate for me and Vance making a go of things, but she doesn't do well when people around her are stressing. And I'm sure she doesn't believe I'm not stressing.

I don't blame her. I don't believe me either.

It's seven-forty, and I haven't heard a peep from him since his last message. So far, he's only ten minutes late, which really is nothing, but the silence, the not knowing, is stressing me—just a little.

"He'll be here," she says. "You said he found that girl from that jerk's tattoo, right?"

Her serious tone startles me. "Uh, yeah, that's what he said."

"Then he's working," she continues. "He's probably talking to her right now, finding out everything he needs to know about that Chad guy."

I nod again, not sure what else to say, and flick the switch on my hair dryer, bending back over. She's right. I shouldn't be stressing. I have no reason to worry. Vance will be here at some point and we'll go out.

He isn't going to change his mind.

He isn't going to get bored.

He isn't ...

Okay, enough.

Enough doubting.

Enough stressing.

Enough.

Kim finishes straightening up my cosmetics and hair products, lining them by size along the edge of the mirror. She's stalling, I think, waiting around so I won't be here alone.

It's pointless, but sweet.

Things have been relatively quiet since Sunday and aside from Vance hanging around and the constant updates on Chad, life's been moving on, getting back to some semblance of normal since the tire incident.

But even if it weren't, Vance is still monitoring my house. There's no need for her or Jimmy to wait around, just in case something happens.

"You don't have to hang around," I say, turning off the hair dryer once more and setting it down on the countertop beside her. "Go have fun. I'm fine here. Promise."

"I know you are," she says and lets out a deep, theatrical sigh, before she hops down and wraps her arms around me in a tight hug. "Try not to stress too much, okay? He'll—"

A shrill ring echoes through the room, stopping her mid-sentence. I snatch up my phone, catching sight of Vance's name on the screen before I hit the button, answering it tentatively. "Hello?"

"Piper," he says in a low voice, "something's come up. Gonna have to postpone dinner."

His words slam into me, and I stiffen, turning away from Kim so she won't see the sudden disappointment climbing up my throat. I knew it. I just knew something like this was going to happen.

"Oh, uh ... okay, sure," I say quietly. "No problem, maybe another time or not, whatever."

"Hey," he says sharply. "What was that?"

I freeze.

From behind me I hear Kim shuffle a step, and then mutter something as her hand squeezes my shoulder. I shrug it off and stick a finger in my ear, ignoring her and focusing my attention on Vance.

"What was what?" I ask hesitantly.

"Another time or not, whatever?" he says and sighs. "Not sure what you're thinking right now, freckles, but don't think you can get rid of me that easy. I'm not going anywhere anytime soon."

I laugh nervously, not sure what to say to that. "Uh, I just ... I thought that ..." I sigh, frustrated. "Never mind."

"Good," he says. "So aren't you going to ask me what came up?"

I stall at those words. "Uh, okay ... What came up?"

"I talked to Trixie, and I think she's hiding Chad," he says. "Jase and Wes are positioned by her house now, watching for him. I should be there, too, but I thought you might be up for a stakeout. I know it's not the steak dinner I promised you, but how do you feel about hanging out with me in my truck tonight?"

My response is immediate. "Are you kidding me? Of course I want to."

He lets out a light laugh, the sound making me smile. "I figured you'd be on board, but I gotta warn you, it's gonna be a long night, and probably boring as fuck."

I laugh. Boring? I doubt that. I can't imagine any time with Vance that could possibly be boring. "I'm in. When do we leave?"

"Right now," he says, laughing again. "I'll be in your driveway in less than ten minutes. Be ready, yeah?"

Less than ten minutes? Before I can respond, the line goes

dead. Call disconnected. I stand there hesitating, contemplating, clutching my phone tightly.

Holy crap. A stakeout. Right now. With Vance.

This is ... exciting.

I'm excited.

"What's going on?"

I jump, turning to face Kim. Her brow furrows as she looks at me.

"I forgot you were here."

She makes a face at me, waving a hand dramatically. "Seriously? How can you possibly forget all of this? I'm hurt. I'm totally hurt."

"I'm going on a stakeout with Vance," I blurt. "He's going to be here to pick me up in less than ten minutes."

"Sounds fun," she says, laughing dryly. She regards me curiously for a moment, her eyes scanning me from head-to-toe. "Um ... you might want to get dressed then, Pipes."

My eyes widen as I look down at the towel wrapped around my body. Less than ten minutes. That's all I have.

Oh, crap.

Tearing out of the bathroom, I'm vaguely aware of Kim following, and snickering, behind me as I lunge for my closet, yanking it open. I rummage through my clothes, pulling out shirts and holding them up, only to toss them aside, searching for ... I don't even know. What do you wear for a stakeout? Comfy or sexy? Something in between?

I don't have a clue.

"Skinny jeans," Kim says as she comes up beside me and pushes me out of the way. She shifts through the hangers, pushing items aside. She knows exactly what she's looking for, and seconds later, she tugs a pair of jeans off a hanger, turns back to me, and holds them up with a satisfied smile on her lips. "These ones."

My brow furrows. "Are you sure? I was thinking—"

"I'm sure," she says, interrupting me. "I've seen the way he checks out your ass when you wear skinny jeans, specifically these ones."

Kim shoves the dark denim pants into my hands, before diving back into the closet, pulling out a basic white ribbed tank top, and tosses it at me.

I catch it, scrunching my nose as I hold it up. "A tank?"

Kim laughs, elbowing me playfully. "Trust me, will you? I know my cousin. Simple is sexy and besides," she shrugs, "you're going to be stuck in a truck all night. Comfy is good, too."

"Right," I say. "Skinny jeans and a tank it is."

Tossing the clothes onto the bed, I start for my dresser, and then stall, as the house alarm lets off a string of beeps instigated by the motion detectors, and then Jimmy shouts, "Pipes, Vance is here!"

"No, no, no," I chant, rushing over to my dresser, and tugging open the top drawer.

There's no way it's been ten minutes.

Kim laughs, casting me an amused look as she walks past me, heading for the door. "Get dressed. I'll stall him."

I mumble a thanks that I'm certain she doesn't hear as she closes the door behind her. Dropping my towel, I quickly slip on a pair of lime green lace panties and matching bra, and then I rush back over to my bed and wiggle into my pants, zipping and buttoning.

I tug on my tank as I move into the bathroom, taking a deep breath before diving into my make-up bag, shifting through the minimal contents. I've never been one to wear a lot of make-up, usually just a touch of blush and gloss, maybe some eyeliner and mascara when I'm feeling daring, but today, I wish I had some foundation. The bruising running from my cheekbone up into my hairline is turning that nasty greenish-yellow, and some cover-up would do wonders for it.

I swipe on some gloss, and spritz on some coconut body spray, before running my hands through my hair, fluffing it up. It's still a little damp, but it'll have to do, because I'm officially out of time.

Heading back into my room, I grab my things, stuffing my cell phone into my purse, and nearly sprint out of the room, jogging down the hallway. My footsteps falter as I round the corner into the empty living room, and I pause completely when my eyes come in contact with Vance through the window.

He's outside, leaning against Kim's car, one arm propped on the roof as he talks with her and Jimmy through the open window. He's wearing his usual uniform of jeans and a tee, laughing at something Kim is saying.

Jesus, he looks good.

He always looks so good.

My heart stalls a beat at the sight of his grin, before kicking into high gear as the butterflies in my belly try to take flight. My feet start to move again, though slower this time, as I step toward the door, setting the alarm to *away* as I pass the panel, and quickly lock up.

Vance pushes off the car, moving a few steps in my direction, as I step away from the door, his eyes flicking over me.

"Hey." I lift my hand, offering a little wave as I cross the driveway. "Sorry for the wait."

He smirks, but remains quiet for a moment, staring at me with an intensity that makes my cheeks blush and my knees weak as I walk toward him, before he finally lifts his chin and says, "Hey, Piper. You ready to go?"

"I, uh, I … I guess so," I stammer foolishly, blushing again and feeling all flustered by his intense gaze, as I stop in front of him.

He chuckles under his breath, his eyes scanning me over once more, and he leans over, placing a quick but firm kiss on my lips.

I gasp, startled by the unexpected kiss, blinking up at him as he pulls away. I'm not sure I'm ever going to get used to this … this …

Ugh. I don't even know what this is.

I don't know what we are.

I don't know what he's doing or what he's looking for.

But he does this a lot, kisses me whenever he feels like it, and each time it feels new, feels different.

And each time, no matter how quick or intense, it's a shock to my system, making my heart thrum and my knees weak.

He chuckles at me, before saying a quick goodbye to Kim and Jimmy, and then he strolls over to the passenger side of his truck, opening the door for me.

"Wow," Kim whispers, gaping. "When the hell did he become a gentleman?"

I let out a sharp bark of laughter, shrugging a shoulder as I whisper, "I don't have a clue, but I'm not going to complain."

Starting up her car, Kim shakes her head, staring at her cousin as he stares at me, waiting for me to get in. "This is just ... odd," she says, putting the car in gear.

Jimmy laughs, patting her shoulder. "Don't worry, Kimmy. One day you'll have your very own badass opening doors for you, too."

Kim rolls her eyes, and I laugh.

Vance watches me curiously as I turn away from Kim, still laughing. He cocks a questioning brow as I hop into the truck, though he doesn't ask, shutting my door and walking around to the driver's side to get in.

Starting up the truck, he stalls for a moment looking at me, his hand on the gear shift.

"What do you feel like for supper? It's gotta be something quick, though, something we can take with us."

"Anything," I say. "I'm game for whatever you feel like."

He lets out a laugh, the sound easing some of my nerves, as he puts the truck in reverse and backs onto the street. "Pita Den."

"Ooo, I love that place."

He cuts his eyes to me, his dark ones twinkling with mirth. "I know," he says. "Chicken Cesar pita, half dressing on whole wheat."

"How did you ..." I start, and then stall, shaking my head. "Jesus, did Kim keep anything a secret from you?"

He laughs. "Not likely."

"I'm definitely going to reconsider my choice in best friends when I get home," I mutter, leaning back in the seat, scowling.

Vance snorts, shaking his head, amused. He says nothing about my comment, though, not that he has to. The smirk says more than enough.

He thinks I'm full of shit.

He's not wrong.

Kim may not be the best at keeping secrets, but she's there when it counts, and really, that's all that matters.

"You get caught up with work?" he asks after a moment, cutting his eyes to me briefly, before focusing back on the road.

"Almost," I say. "I sent off the last draft today. Once it's approved I just need to make a few tweaks and send the final files."

He nods, hesitating as he quickly glances over at me again. "Elena's gonna be home on Saturday and we're planning a barbeque for her, nothing big, just a little welcome home kind of thing with the guys. You should come."

He wants me to go to Elena's welcome home barbeque?

"I ... I don't know," I say hesitantly. "I don't even know her. She probably doesn't want some stranger hanging around when she hasn't seen you guys in weeks."

"Nonsense," he says. "She'll love having you there."

He says it so confidently that I can't think of a reason not to, so I shrug. "Okay, sounds fun."

It takes ten minutes to get to Pita Den. I wait in the truck as Vance runs in to grab our food. It doesn't take him long, less than five minutes, before he's back in the truck, and we're on the road again.

As we drive, Vance fills me in on his entirely unhelpful meeting with Trixie Starr.

She's a nurse.

He's pretty sure she knows who I am, though I don't have a clue how.

She's not giving up anything on her man.

As far as leads go, she seems like a dead end to me, but Vance is confident that Chad Miller is hanging around, most likely staying at her place, hence the stakeout.

We end up at a park, across the street and down a little from

Trixie's house. From our vantage point, we can see the front of the house clearly, as well as Jase, who's parked at the curb a block and a half down. I can't see Wes from our spot, but we passed him on a side street on our way into the park, keeping an eye on the back of the house.

"What happens now?" I ask, settling my pita on my knees and unwrapping it.

Vance glances at me, amusement flashing in his eyes. "We wait."

I thought he'd been joking.

I was hoping he was joking.

I thought maybe there'd be gadgets to play with, cool spy equipment to test out. But as I sit in the truck, fiddling with the radio, I realize he meant it. All we can do now is wait.

Hours pass. Long hours of nothing.

The sun sets, and the house we're watching stays quiet. No one comes in or out. No one turns on a light or passes by a window.

Vance and I talk and talk and talk, about nothing and everything. Parents: his are still around, living in Florida. Siblings: he doesn't have any. Favorite food: anything barbequed. We hit topic after topic, and not unexpected, he already knows most of my answers, and I only manage to surprise him once when I confess that I've never eaten fish because I don't like the way it smells.

Jase and Wes send periodic text messages. Updates, I guess, though there really hasn't been anything to update—yet.

But overall, this whole stakeout thing is somewhat ... boring. I guess he meant that, too, when he said it.

Sighing, I stretch in my seat, turning to face him. "What exactly is your plan, you know, if we see him?"

Vance cocks an eyebrow at me. "You don't already know?"

"No. I mean, I can guess, but I don't really know, you know?"

He chuckles and leans back in the seat, resting his head on the headrest. "Let's hear your guess."

"Um ..." I smile bashfully, fluttering my lashes. "You'll use your badassness to scare him into leaving me alone and maybe, hopefully pay for all the damages?"

He lets out a loud laugh and my eyes narrow slightly.

"You think my badassness is scary?"

"Uh, yeah," I say, cutting him an incredulous look. "And so did that guy at the apartment the day Kim and I moved in."

"He was an asshole," he mutters. "A punk with no goddamn respect, and if I recall correctly, it was him grabbing a handful of your ass that started the whole thing."

I grimace. He's right. I was carrying a large vase, one my mother made before she died, struggling with the lobby door, when some guy came up behind me. He smacked my ass as he all but shoved me out of the way, and I dropped the vase, shattering it.

Of course, Vance saw the whole thing.

He'd just pulled up and gotten out of his truck when I shrieked out my surprise, and I swear it took only seconds— mere seconds—for him to have the guy, who wasn't small by any means, spewing out apology after apology.

It was at that moment, I dubbed Vance badass hottie, and five minutes later, I found out he was Kim's cousin.

"Fine, you're not going to use your badassness," I say. "So what's the real plan then?"

"We're gonna ask him a few questions," he says, pausing as he chuckles again. "Then we'll turn him over to Cruz."

I stare at him for a moment, blinking a few times.

"Huh," I say. "I suppose that could work, too."

Vance chuckles and I roll my eyes, leaning forward once again to fiddle with the radio, flipping through the stations. I switch through them all once, twice, three times, before a familiar song hits my ears, causing me to laugh.

It's that song.

The one from the bar.

The one Vance watched me dance to.

Instinctively, I start to move in my seat, wiggling my hips against the leather, bobbing my head with the beat.

Glancing at Vance, I laugh a little as I see the recognition flare behind his eyes. He reaches over, turning it up, his gaze glued to me.

I'm smiling.

I'm singing.

I'm moving to the beat.

I'm having fun.

He watches me intently, smirking, and I feel my entire body heat under his gaze. I wonder if he knows what he's doing to me as his gaze rakes over me, dropping to my mouth, staring at my lips as though the thought of kissing me suddenly consumes him.

And then the song ends, and his mouth kicks up in a sexy one-sided grin. "Fuck, I love watching you do that," he mutters, licking his lips. "Gotta download that song so I can play it again and again and again."

I grin, shaking my head. "Already done. I've got it on my phone."

My response makes him laugh. He leans into me, and I think he's going to kiss me, but he pauses mere inches from my mouth, and whispers, "Good to know."

I don't know whether to laugh, or growl in frustration. I start to tilt toward him, wanting that darn kiss, when I stall, a movement in my peripheral vision catching my attention.

"Vance?" I whisper, licking my suddenly dry lips.

"Yeah?"

"Is that him?" I ask, pulling back abruptly. "Jesus, I think it is. He's actually here."

Chapter Fourteen

Vance

In hindsight, bringing Piper along on a stakeout may not have been the best idea.

I'm trying to pay attention to everything going on around us, to stay vigilant and spot the asshole, and nab him before he can do any more damage, but the girl sitting beside me keeps distracting me. A light touch, a smile, a laugh; it's all a distraction.

A fucking incredible distraction.

From my seat in the truck, I can see three blocks down in both directions and most of the park around us. It's a few minutes after eleven o'clock, and most of the houses are already dark. The street itself is bathed in a muted glow from the streetlights.

Piper's abandoned her spot, pressed up against the center console leaning toward me, to hover at the far side of the truck, staring out the window and pointing into the darkness.

Following her outstretched finger, every muscle seizes in my body the moment I spot Chad Miller. There he is, moving through the park toward us, ducking in and out of the shadows.

Jesus, I almost missed him, distracted by Piper. But I know it's him. I recognize him from the mug shot.

He knows we're looking for him, I think, as I watch him dart from tree to tree still a good forty feet from us. Trixie tipped him off, most likely. He's sticking to the shadows, though the basic white cotton tee he's wearing makes him stand out.

I reach for my phone, snagging it off the dashboard, when Piper shuffles in her seat, her hand shooting for the door.

"Hey." I stop Piper before she pops the door open and turn her to face me, my hands on her arms. Her muscles tense as I pull her back toward me. "Where are you going?"

Her eyes lift to mine and she blinks, a frown spreading across her lips. "You said we were going to ask him some questions."

I stifle a groan at that. Yep, bringing her along was definitely not a good idea.

"We, as in me, Jase, and Wes," I clarify. "And in order to do that, I need to let the guys know that he's here. But you ... You're gonna keep that hot little ass of yours planted right here in this seat."

She gapes at me, as though she thinks I'm fucking with her, but I'm not. The guy has already tried to hurt her once. There's no goddamn way I'm letting her get within spitting distance of him tonight.

"I'm coming with you," she says, her voice all whiplash warning. "I'm part of this."

This time, I can't stifle the groan that slips out, but I don't humor her with any further of a response, as I quickly tap out a message to Jase and Wes, letting them know Chad's in the park, closing in on the street, and that he's acting skittish.

He's expecting us—or someone.

He's watching.

He's waiting.

They both come back with messages instantly, and my mind works fast as we quickly strategize. The park is too open, too many places for him to run, too many chances for him to get away. My eyes dart around in the darkness, looking for a place to corner him, but the only thing that stands out is the small picket fence surrounding Trixie's yard.

It's not ideal, too open and public for my taste, but it'll have to do.

Piper's silent as we send quick messages back and forth, her gaze shifting between me and Chad as he slowly makes his way along the edge of the grassy area toward the house, choosing to stick close to the minimal tree coverage instead of cutting a straight line to his target.

He creeps closer—fifteen feet away from the street at most—moving right in front of the truck, and I nearly laugh when he barely spares us a glance.

He's oblivious, it seems.

Or perhaps it's not us he's trying so hard to hide from.

"What are you waiting for?" Piper asks as I shove my phone into my pocket. "He's going to get away."

"He won't get away," I say, keeping my eyes on the target. "I'm waiting for the guys to get into position. We're gonna corner him by the fence so he can't take off running."

"Oh." She looks out the windshield, her gaze scanning the street, and she exhales a long impatient breath. "Where are they?"

I fight a smile at her brisk tone. "Jase is moving along the trees to our right." I point him out, and then pause, waiting, eyes scanning for Wes. "And Wes just rounded the corner on our left."

Chad moves another few steps, and then stalls, hesitating. His eyes linger for a moment on Jase, and then Wes, as they move indifferently down the sidewalk toward him. He must not think they are a threat, because he shoves his hands in his pockets, and then ducks out of the shadows, keeping his gaze on the ground.

Turning to Piper, I give her a look. "Stay here, yeah?"

"Vance …" She huffs out a breath and folds her arms over her chest, pouting dramatically. "I just … I want to hear what he has to say … why he's doing this to me."

"Fair enough," I say. "Why don't you let me find that out and I'll let you know later."

She opens her mouth to speak, but before she can respond, I reach for her, tangling my hand in her hair at her nape, and tug her to me. Tilting my head, leaning further into her, I pause with my lips just a breath away from hers.

"You need to stay put and out of sight, Piper," I say against her lips, my eyes locked with hers. "Can't deal with him and worry about you at the same time."

She must read the resoluteness in my tone, because she nods erratically and then takes a deep breath, swallowing hard as though clearing a sudden lump in her throat. "Okay."

I press my lips to hers, kissing her quickly.

She kisses me back urgently—aggressively—pouring all her frustration and anger into it.

She's angry with me for telling her to stay put.

She's frustrated that she knows I'm right.

The kiss only lasts a second before I pull away, and get out of the truck, closing the door with a quiet click.

Chad is halfway across the street when I hit the sidewalk. I stroll toward him, in no rush, closing in behind him. Jase and Wes are about ten feet away, moving in on either side, boxing him in.

My gaze flickers toward Piper, and I breathe a sigh of relief when I see her still sitting in the truck, before picking up my pace.

I hit the middle of the street as Chad steps up onto the opposite sidewalk. His head is still down. He's not paying any attention to us, rushing to the driveway of his girlfriend's house.

"Yo, Chad," Wes says, keeping his voice low and steady as he greets him. "Glad I finally caught up with you, man."

Chad freezes, and then spins around, frantically taking a few steps back, nearly backing right into Jase. "Who the fuck are you?"

"Name's Wes," he says, and then jerks his chin toward me. "That's Vance, and the guy behind you is Jase."

Our presence unnerves him. I can see it on his face as he swivels, taking us in, eyes darting around as though looking for a way out.

He looks like a rat caught in a maze.

His head turns and his gaze latches onto the small fence behind him. I can see the exact moment he decides to try to jump it, the idea flashing loudly across his expression. He turns, his hands reaching for the top of the waist-high structure, and I open my mouth to stop him, but Jase beats me to it.

"Don't even try," Jase grinds out, his voice cold and harsh. "If you make me fuckin' chase you, you won't like what happens when I catch you."

Chad hesitates for a moment, considering whether or not to test Jase's threat no doubt, before he slowly lowers his hands and turns back to us. "Look, I don't ... I don't have the money on me, but I can get it."

My brow furrows. "Money?"

"It's in the house." Chad glances behind him. "Just back off and I can get it for you right now."

From the corner of my eye, I see Jase's forehead crease with confusion. He casts a disbelieving look my way, arching a questioning brow, and I shrug. I don't know what he's talking about. I haven't heard a word from any of my contacts about him owing anyone.

"Relax," I say. "We're not here for money. We just have a few questions for you is all."

Chad tenses, his body rigid. He stares at me, studying my face, deciding if he should believe me or not.

Five seconds pass ... ten ... fifteen, before something like recognition passes across his eyes, and he lets out a startled laugh. "Shit. You're those private investigators that were talking to Trixie earlier, aren't you?"

Wes nods. "Yeah, that's us."

Chad's expression shifts, twisting with rage. He takes a step toward Wes, his hands curling into fists.

He looks like he's gonna take a swing, but so does Wes.

They glare at each other for a tick.

"You assholes caused a lot of shit for me," Chad snarls, his glare shifting between us. "Filling Trixie's head with lies about tormenting some Piper chick, telling her I vandalized this chick's house, and the bit about the truck ... That girl paid me to loosen the bolts for her."

My skin prickles as I listen to him, and something ugly coils inside me that I quickly try to unwind before it wraps me up too tight and I lose sight of what we're really doing here.

I want to punch him.

Fuck. I want to beat him until he bleeds.

I pull in a deep breath, and slowly let it out. "You saying someone paid you to loosen the tire on that truck?"

"Yeah," he says right away, taking a step back. "Someone paid me."

There's no hesitation. No shifting eyes, or twitches.

I think he's telling the goddamn truth.

Taking another deep breath, I ask, "And you didn't see anything wrong with that?"

He shrugs. "It was her truck. She said the tire was flat and she couldn't get the bolts off. Paid me a hundred bucks to help her out."

"You actually see that flat tire?" Jase asks.

"I don't know, man," he says. "I was wasted. I loosened the bolts, offered to change the tire, too, but she said she could handle it, so I took the cash and took off."

"What about—"

"You're lying."

I stall, mid-question, and turn around, staring at Piper. Her eyes are watering, her cheeks, nearly as red as her hair. She stares at Chad, her body so tense it's as though she's holding her breath, fighting to keep her fury within, but she can't contain it all. It leaks out, dribbling down her cheek in a tear.

She looks as though she's ready to burst, though whether it'll come out in tears or a storm of fury, I don't know.

What I do know is that I need her to go back to where she was, before either of those things happen.

"Go back to the truck, Piper," I say, fighting to keep my tone calm. "You don't want to do this right now."

She doesn't respond, and she doesn't go back to the truck.

No, instead she comes closer, her fiery eyes glued to Chad and her hands curling into white knuckled fists, hissing, "I never asked you to touch my truck. I never paid you to loosen my tires. Tell the truth, you asshole!"

I stare at her for a tick, feeling my jaw go slack.

She looks vicious, so far removed from the sweet and quiet girl I know.

"The girl I helped out was a blonde," Chad says slowly, his tone almost hesitant as though he's worried she might actually attack him. "Trixie told me about your accident and I'm really fucking sorry, but I swear, I thought I was helping someone."

Piper's eyes narrow at those words, and she stares at him.

And stares.

And stares at him some more.

"You were caught on video that night by my truck," she says quietly. "The police are looking for you and I'm going to call them now. You're going to tell them everything you know. Everything you remember about her. If you do that, then I'll make sure these guys are going to work there asses off to clear your name."

Jase lets out a startled laugh, and Wes gapes at her.

I merely grin, shaking my head.

"I can do that," Chad says without hesitation.

Un-fuckin'-believable.

Piper

I don't call the police.

I don't need to.

Moments after I make the statement, Detective Cruz pulls up. One of the guys must have called him before they even got out of their vehicle.

It takes a little over thirty minutes for us to fill him in, answering questions, explaining the situation, before he lets me and the guys go, and hauls Chad off to the station to collect his statement.

Vance doesn't say a word to me as we get into his truck. My heart is pounding so fast I can feel each beat, each thump, in the tips of my fingers. He's in a peculiar mood, not quite angry, not entirely not.

I don't know what to make of it.

As soon as my seatbelt is in place, he pulls out of the park and onto the street. His eyes stay focused on the windshield, not even glancing at the mirrors as he drives, keeping his neck tense as though he doesn't want to risk looking in my direction.

I think I screwed up.

Big time.

I'm just not sure if it's because I got out of the truck when he explicitly told me not to, or if it's because I offered his help to Chad without asking him first.

I'm not sure it matters either way.

Five minutes pass in silence, before I start to fidget.

Another two minutes, and I feel as though I'm going to scream or perhaps even cry, just to make some noise and release my pent up anxiety.

"I know you're mad at me," I say, unable to contain my nerves any longer. It's been awhile since I've felt this nervous around him. I guess I've grown used to him, comfortable with him, but now, with the odd mood he's in, I'm not sure what to do with myself.

It just feels ... different somehow.

He feels different, uptight and relaxed all at the same time.

"I'm not mad," he says. "Shocked, maybe a little frustrated, but not mad."

"You seem mad," I counter. "If it's about me getting out of the truck, I'm sorry, but I just couldn't sit there and watch. I couldn't do it."

"I know," he says. "And like I said, I'm not mad."

I turn to him confused, and he gives me a look that I think is supposed to be reassuring, but it only manages to cause more unease.

"If Chad needs help clearing his name, I'll pay for it."

He lets out a sharp laugh. "Jesus, Piper, it's all good. Stop worrying so damn much."

"Then what is it?" I snap, frustrated. "What's eating at you?"

He cuts his eyes to me and frowns, before turning his focus back onto the road. "Thought we had him," he mumbles after a moment. "Thought this shit was gonna be over, but all we've got now is that the girl behind everything is blonde. We're no closer now than we were a week ago."

It's a fair statement, but I don't know what to say. I'm trying to stay positive. I want to believe the quietness of the last week means it's over.

My stalker is gone.

The vandalism is over.

But I think, somewhere deep down, I know it's not. I just don't want to give voice to the worry. I don't want to make it real.

Instead of babbling on and making the tension worse, I turn back to the window, watching the houses fly past as we drive toward my place.

Vance doesn't say anything when we arrive, only pulls his truck over to the curb, not even bothering to pull into the driveway. He doesn't even look at me, just stares out the windshield, his entire body tense behind the wheel.

It burns.

I turn in my seat, getting ready to ask him if he's okay, if everything's okay between us, when his eyes finally meet mine. The look he gives me makes my question freeze in my throat, the dark shadows in his eyes making me suck in a sharp breath.

"If I ask you to stay in the truck, will you listen to me this time?" he asks, his voice deathly calm.

My stomach coils and sinks. "I, uh, I … what's wrong?"

He sighs. "That's what I thought," he says, and hesitates for a long moment. "Look at the driveway, freckles."

The tone of his voice freaks me out, scares me so much that I want to refuse.

I don't want to.

I can't help it.

I have to look.

I look.

My heart races faster than before, so frenzied it hurts my chest as I slowly turn toward my house, catching sight of my driveway.

I blink.

I blink again.

And then I gasp.

The driveway just beyond the sidewalk is now marred with foul orange spray paint with even fouler words written across the surface. A poster board sign on a spike, jabbed into the lawn has the word *whore* scrawled across it, another with the word *slut*, and another with the words *you were warned*.

My hand is shaking as I lift it to my mouth, my entire body rattling against the seat, as I fight back the tears that threaten to fall.

This can't be happening.

This can't be real.

My vision blurs with tears and I squeeze my eyes shut. I will not cry. I will not let this get to me. It's not the first time my property has been ruined. It doesn't matter what the words say.

It doesn't matter.

It doesn't matter.

But it does matter. It matters a lot.

Vance puts an arm around my shoulder, tugging me to his chest. I resist at first. I know the comfort will be my undoing. But he's not having it. His hand comes up to cup the back of my head, tucking my head up under his chin, and my resistance breaks.

I suck in a breath.

And another.

And then I cry.

It's not pretty.

There are no cute little sniffles or hiccups.

It's messy and ugly. I'm gasping for breath, sucking in mouthfuls, but getting so little air my lungs scream and burn.

I let it all out. I don't really have a choice in the matter. My body has taken over, determined to purge all the grief and fear and pain I've been bottling up since this whole mess began.

It's not until my shaking stops and my tears dry up that Vance loosens his hold on me and says, "We need to call the cops."

Chapter Fifteen

Piper

"Can you explain to me how none of these cameras caught the person who did this?" I ask, waving around one of the crudely painted signs as Vance opens the garage door.

He cuts his eyes to me, regarding me peculiarly, before he lets out a long sigh, ending it with the word, "Piper."

That's it.

That's all he says.

He strolls over to me, reaching around me, his hand coming to rest on my hip, as the other reaches for the sign, gently taking it from my hand and tossing it into the garage behind him. He says nothing, but his thoughts are there, written in his dark eyes and in the frown marring his face.

He's just as angry as I am.

He's also getting frustrated that I keep asking the same question.

But I can't help it.

I'm shaky and edgy, the tears and anger making me feel an odd mix of hyped-up and exhausted. The police have come and gone, snapping pictures of the damage and taking down an incident report. They went through the empty video file for tonight, discussed with Vance where the cameras are located, and how far on the property someone has to be to trigger them.

I listened to everything, walked through the paces with them, testing the cameras and determining where the person must have stood based on the direction of the paint spray and lack of video feed, but the problem is that no matter how many times I hear the explanation, I still don't understand and it's making me crazy.

"It's just that I don't understand," I say quietly, suddenly feeling an overwhelming need to backtrack and explain myself. "How did the person know about them? How did they know if they stood on the sidewalk the cameras wouldn't catch them?"

He squeezes my hip, his frown softening slightly. "Piper ..." he sighs. "Look, I can't tell you anything more than I already have. The cameras are set to record your property. They're on motion sensors, just like you wanted. If the sensors aren't tripped, they won't record. If a person doesn't come on the property—"

"But they painted my property," I interrupt, anxiously glancing down the driveway, catching sight of the paint once again. "The cameras should have picked that up."

My words make him hesitate. He pauses, and stares down at me with a peculiar mix of adoration and irritation, but he doesn't speak.

I'm not sure what to do, or say. I know I'm being a pain in the ass, but I can't rein it in, so I just stare back at him, working hard at keeping the swirl of emotions off my face.

After a moment, Vance sighs. "They painted from the sidewalk. You saw that, how the words run between the sidewalk and your driveway. Spray paint ain't enough to trigger a sensor, honey."

"Why did you install motion activated cameras?"

The hostility in my voice makes me cringe and my stomach sinks. Ugh, I sound bitchy and accusatory, not curious as it was meant to be.

I just want to understand.

I want to know if I need something more—something better.

Vance groans in frustration, and lets go of my hip, taking a step back. He says nothing, just stares at me for a moment, before he turns away, shaking his head as he wanders back down the driveway and yanks out another sign.

I stand still, just staring at him as he grabs the rest of the signs, and then stalks back up the driveway, tossing them in the garage, before walking away from me once more, heading over to his truck still parked at the curb. My stomach coils as he jumps in and starts it up, the sudden fear that he's going to just drive away, without even saying goodbye, surges through me.

I don't want him to go.

I don't want to be alone.

But it's more than that, too. I want him to stay because I like having him here; I like how I feel when he's in my space. I want him to stay because he's Vance and I've wanted him for so long I barely remember a time before him.

My heart stalls as the truck pulls away from the curb, and then kicks up, pounding in my chest when he pulls into the driveway, parking right in front of the garage where I'm standing. He doesn't turn off the truck right away, and he doesn't get out. Hesitating with his hand on the steering wheel, his gaze sweeps over me. I can't make out his expression, the headlights causing a glare, but I can feel his eyes on me, the intensity of them searing my skin.

My body flushes with embarrassment from the way I've been acting, and I know my nervousness is written all over my face, as I round the truck, heading for the driver's side.

Vance cuts the engine as I start to move, opens the door, and folds out of the vehicle. He meets me at the front fender, pausing right in front of me, so close that I nearly take a step back, and it takes every ounce of strength I have to hold my ground under his irate stare.

I open my mouth, ready to spew out a jumbled apology, but he speaks before I can get a single word out. "Have I given you any reason not to trust me, Piper?" he asks. "Any reason at all to think I'm not doing everything I can to figure this shit out for you?"

"No," I say quietly, forcing myself not to recoil from the bite in his tone. "No, you haven't."

"Then trust me," he says. "Trust that I put in the best security system. Know that the cameras I used are exactly what you need. Believe that I'll find the person doing this. If you want me to do a new install, rip everything out and upgrade it, I will. I'll do whatever it takes for you to trust me here, to believe that I'll fix this shit for you."

"No, I don't want you to do that," I say. "I just ... I'm sorry. I'm stressed and I'm taking it out on you, and that's not cool. None of this is your fault."

He leans into me then and kisses my forehead, wrapping his arms tightly around me, hugging me close. I don't know how long we stand there, before he finally pulls away, grinning down at me. "You should probably head in," he says. "Try to get some sleep, put this shit behind you, yeah?"

"Will you stay with me?" I ask right away, my voice soft, barely audible even to my own ears, but he hears me. I can see it in his eyes, the flare of heat, the subtle flicker of uncertainty. The odd mix has my skin heating and my nerves jumping.

"Is that okay?" I ask when he doesn't respond. "Can you stay with me tonight and, uh, maybe hold me?"

He nods. "Yeah, freckles, I can do that."

Vance lets go of me then, moving over to the garage, closing and locking it up, and then comes back to me, taking my hand.

He pulls me into the house, locking the door and setting the alarm as he tugs me down the hallway to my room. For a fleeting second, my nerves resurface as he closes the bedroom door behind us, but they don't last. Exhaustion is winning the battle on my emotions, and all I want is to curl up under the blankets and put this day behind me.

Grabbing a sleep shirt and new panties from my dresser, I dip into the bathroom as Vance slips back out of the room, mumbling something about brushing his teeth. I get changed, and do my bedtime routine, brushing my teeth and washing my face, before venturing back in the bedroom to find Vance stripped down to his boxers, fiddling with the monitor on my dresser.

I stare at him momentarily frozen as I get my first look at him without clothes. My body flushes as I take in all that tanned skin and hard muscle.

Jesus, he's gorgeous.

"Get in bed, Piper," he says, drawing my attention from the solid length of his backside. "I'll be there in a minute."

"What are you doing?" I ask curiously, watching as he taps the screen, bringing up what looks like the control panel.

"Adjusting the volume," he says. "Don't want it waking you up when Jimmy stumbles in."

Huh. I didn't even know that was an option.

"But what if something happens?" I ask, crossing over to my bed and climbing in. "What if the person comes back tonight?"

"I'm a light sleeper," he says. "I'll hear it."

He turns to me as he finishes, smiling as he flicks off the light and strolls over to the bed. The mattress shifts as he climbs in beside me. His hand seeks me out, wrapping around my waist and pulling me to him, his chest pressing close against my back. The motion eases the remaining strands of anxiety from before, and I sigh, settling into him.

"You okay?" he asks quietly.

I probably shouldn't be. I think it would be reasonable enough to still be freaking out, to be twisted up, upset and unnerved.

But I'm not.

I feel comfortable and warm and safe.

"Yeah," I say. "I'm okay."

He nuzzles my neck, kissing the skin there lightly as he pulls me closer, deeper into his arms, settling in behind me. It doesn't take long for sleep to catch me, dragging me down into a dark nothingness.

I sleep deeply and soundly right through the night. When I come around much later, I'm greeted with sunlight and silence, instantly aware of how empty the bed feels beside me.

Vance is gone.

Rubbing my eyes, I sit up in bed. His clothes are gone from the bedroom floor; his wallet and phone are no longer sitting on the dresser.

A glance at the clock tells me that it's eleven-thirty in the morning, so I'm not surprised he's gone, but undeniably it stings to realize I'm alone.

Slipping out of bed, I hit the bathroom and pull on a pair of shorts, before venturing out of my room and down the hall, listening for any sounds of life within the house, hoping he's still here somewhere.

Everything is quiet and still, but I smell coffee brewing, so I pad over to the kitchen. When I get there, Vance isn't around, but Jimmy is here, hunched over the counter, watching the coffee brew.

"Morning," I say, strolling past him and grabbing a mug from the cupboard. "Have you been up long?"

"Yeah," he says, his voice quiet and serious. "Since five-thirty."

I laugh, thinking he has to be joking, because Jimmy is not a morning person, but when he turns around to look at me and I see his face, the first thing I notice are his bloodshot eyes and the black circles underneath. "Long night?"

"And morning," he mutters, leaning back against the countertop. He's still wearing the same clothes from yesterday, I notice, as his eyes regard me peculiarly, a smirk turning up his lips. "Wasn't expecting to see a guy coming out of your room this morning. Nearly beat Vance with your lamp when he walked by the couch. Lucky for him, I was still drunk as shit and I fell back down the second I stood up."

I let out a loud laugh and he grimaces, looking back at the coffee pot, glaring at it as though it will make it brew faster. "Oh God, I'm sorry. I should have warned you. I didn't think he'd leave so early."

"He's not gone," Jimmy says. "He's in the garage."

Wait ... What?

"He's in the garage?" I ask, my brow furrowing. "Why is he in the garage?"

Jimmy rolls his eyes, opening his mouth to respond, but I don't wait for his answer, turning away from him and moving through the living room, heading for the door that leads to the garage.

I find Vance winding the garden hose on the reel when I open the door. He looks up and smiles as I tentatively make my way down the steps toward him. "You're awake."

"You are, too," I say. "What are you doing out here?"

He raises an eyebrow, his expression amused as he says, "Just finished washing down the driveway."

I blink at him, dumbfounded, still half asleep and out of it. He washed down my driveway? I don't know what to say. "Um … wow, thank you," I say. "You didn't have to do that."

He laughs at my reaction. "We're taking off for the afternoon. Wanted this done before we leave."

"We're taking off for the afternoon," I parrot, blinking at him again, caught off guard.

He nods. "Yeah, we are."

"Um … where are we going?"

Vance chuckles, shaking his head at my reaction. "You'll see when we get there."

I roll my eyes. He looks so relaxed, sounds so confident that I'm going to just drop everything and follow him blindly.

Most days I think I would.

"I'm supposed to get my stitches out today," I remind him. "The appointment's at twelve-fifteen, so, uh, I can't just take off."

"I remember," he says. "It'll take five minutes to get those stitches out, and then we're gonna go have some fun."

"But it's Friday. What about drinks with the guys?"

He lets out a laugh of disbelief, and steps toward me. "Are you making excuses, Piper? Trying to get out of spending some time with me?"

I laugh as his words strike me, because they sound utterly ridiculous, but my amusement doesn't last long when I notice his dead serious expression. I open my mouth to respond—to say what, I really don't know—but he doesn't give me a chance to speak.

"Because if that's what you're doing, you can forget it," he continues. "Go get dressed while I finish up here. And pack a swimsuit. I'll be there in a few minutes to help you with the picnic."

Chapter Sixteen

Vance

Two and a half hours later, Piper's standing on a dock at the Sacramento Marina, looking down at my boat. I'd taken her to get her stitches out, spending far more time in the waiting room than it did to have the things removed, and she's had a hand in her hair, unconsciously scratching at her fresh scar since we left.

She looks perplexed, chewing on her bottom lip as she takes in the boat. It's nothing overly special—nothing like the sailboat I used to own—just an older cabin cruiser, but the way she's looking at it, fuck if it doesn't make me nervous.

Maybe this was a bad idea.

I probably should have asked her if she was interested in boating before bringing her out here, but damn, I really want her to like it.

Like it as much as I do.

Piper tilts her head, shifting slightly to look back at me. A hint of a smile touches her lips, before morphing into a full-blown grin. "I can't believe you have a boat and I didn't know about it."

I smile at the sound of her anticipation, the knot in my gut slowly unwinding. "You probably didn't know because Kim's not allowed anywhere near it unsupervised."

She turns around, facing me fully, raising her eyebrows in

surprise. "Why is that?"

I chuckle. "She thought it'd be a great idea to take it out and party on it. Cost me nearly five grand in repairs and cleaning when she brought it back."

Shock freezes her in place as she stares at me, stunned for a tick, before her pretty lips turn down in a pout, and she lets out a rueful laugh. "I can't believe she didn't invite me."

"I've had this thing about four years now," I say. "Her party happened a long time before you showed up."

"I've never been on a boat before." She looks back at it. "I've always wanted to. Is it as fun as it looks?"

"Climb on and find out," I say, motioning with my hand for her to hop in.

Hesitantly, she grasps onto my arm, carefully jumping in. Once she's steady, I grab the foam cooler off the dock, following her on board and moving straight to the cockpit, setting the cooler down.

Piper drops her bag on the deck and wanders about the boat, checking out the deck, running her fingers along the seats, as I quickly move around, getting us ready.

After her thorough inspection, she perches on the seat beside the steering wheel, watching me curiously.

Christ, I fuckin' love the way she looks at me, the way her eyes trace over me, as though she's trying to memorize everything about me.

"Jesus, it's hot out today," she says, pulling her long hair off her neck and holding it in a bunch on top of her head.

"It won't be bad once we get out on the water," I tell her. "You can change in the cabin, though, while I get us moving, if you want."

Piper hesitates for a tick, seemingly unsure if she wants to put on her swimsuit, but the heat eventually wins out, and she grabs her bag, disappearing into the cabin. She's only gone for a few minutes, just long enough for me to untie the boat, and get us out and away from the docks, before she emerges from the cabin, wearing a barely there bikini. It's white, tied to her with blue strings at her hips, and around her neck and back.

My eyes instinctively scan her body, taking in all the curves and dips and dimples. The material of her swimsuit covers her most intimate places, but otherwise leaves little shielded from my sight.

So damn pretty.

My cock perks up, hardening once again within the constraints of my jeans. I've been in a state of semi-hard since seeing her again, and after last night, curling up with her and feeling her soft warmth pressed against me, seeing her in that tiny thing is nearly unbearable to look at and it takes every bit of self-restraint I have to not reach over and haul her to me.

The flush of her cheeks tells me very clearly she's caught me openly checking her out, and the small smile lets me know that she's not unhappy about the way I'm staring. She makes her way over to me, perching on the edge of the seat beside mine.

Piper doesn't say a word. Doesn't ask where we're going or what the plan is. She just sits back, and enjoys the wind and the water as her eyes scan the shoreline, her face split into a wide smile.

It's ... awesome.

We cruise around for a while. Piper laughs and smiles, and although she chats a little, she seems more than content in just experiencing the boat ride.

She doesn't bring up her case. Doesn't question the security system again, or ask what the new plan is.

She just relaxes and seeing her like this, all loose and smiling, makes me feel so goddamn good.

Eventually, I slow down, pulling the boat off to the side of the river. I drop the anchors, and we settle down on the large L-shaped couch at the back of the boat, the cooler settled on the floor between us.

"You know," Piper says, settling in, pulling her legs up under her. "I think this is exactly what I needed. I don't remember ever feeling this relaxed. Not even in Mexico."

I laugh. "We'll have to make this a regular thing then."

She looks at me, a tiny frown tugging her lips. "Do you do this a lot?"

"Do what?" I ask curiously.

"Make picnics and bring girls out here," she asks, her voice hesitant, as though maybe she doesn't actually want to hear the answer.

I stare at Piper.

She stares right back at me.

Jesus, she sounds ... jealous. She looks it, too.

It's a pretty look on her.

Always so damn pretty.

I grin at her, and then pull the lid off the cooler, reaching in and retrieving a beer.

"You're the first," I say, twisting off the cap and handing it to her. "Don't bring too many people out here, actually."

Her eyes widen. "What?"

"You're the first," I say again, reaching over to her, lightly trailing the back of my knuckles along the curve where her neck and shoulder meets. It's a barely there touch, but the contact makes her shiver and blush. "And I've never made a picnic for anyone before you either."

"I, uh, I ..." her blush deepens and her voice wobbles. "Really?"

She's nervous and she takes a long pull from her beer.

"Really," I say, letting my hand fall away, wanting to put her at ease. I reach into the cooler, grabbing a beer for myself, twisting it open.

When I glance back at her, she's staring at me, confused, as though I haven't answered her question at all, so I decide to elaborate.

"This is my getaway, the place I come to clear my head. The guys come out with me every once in a while, but for the most part I keep the boat to myself. It's ... special to me, sacred even. I don't bring just anyone out here."

"So it's a special place," she reiterates, surprised. "*Your* special place."

I take a pull from my beer. "Essentially, yeah."

My response relaxes her, and she beams at me as though being here makes her special, too.

It does.

She is special to me.

"Do you spend a lot of time on the water?"

"Not so much anymore," I say. "But whenever I get a chance, I take her out. I used to have a sailboat, back before I started working with Jase and Wes. Spent the summers on it, going wherever I felt like."

A flicker of surprise passes across her eyes, but she wipes it away quickly, giving me another small smile. "I've thought about getting a boat. It would be cool to spend a summer sailing. My parents did it once and I have all these pictures of them, before us kids were born, on the boat in the Caribbean."

"You should do it," I say. "It's fuckin' amazing, best experience I've ever had."

"Yeah, maybe someday," she says, looking from me to her beer, then back at me, before reaching into the cooler and pulling out the roast beef sandwiches and container of potato salad.

The day speeds away, early afternoon slipping by before I know it. We eat, and talk, joking around and laughing, just like any normal couple.

It's ... odd, and completely unexpected, but I gotta admit, I love it.

Love every second of it.

Our picnic is cleaned up, all the wrappers and containers stuffed back into the cooler, and after a couple beers, Piper stretches herself out on the couch, her head in my lap, soaking up the sun.

She looks so ... happy.

Relaxed.

Content.

Looking down at her, I trace lazy lines across her skin. If it weren't so fucking hot out here, I don't think I'd ever move from this spot. But I'm sweating, and Piper's skin is turning pink, even though she's been lathering on that sunscreen of hers like crazy.

"You're starting to burn," I say. "Let's get you out of the sun for a bit, yeah?"

Piper smiles contentedly up at me. She says nothing as she slips off my lap, standing up and grabbing her beer off the floor, before wandering over toward the steps.

I follow her, flicking on the light and cranking up the air conditioner when we make it inside the cabin.

I expect her to cover up and throw her dress on, but she doesn't, instead choosing to wander around the small cabin in that skimpy little bikini.

It's torture.

The best kind of torture.

She sets her beer down on the table, and runs a hand along the tees and shorts, stacked up on the shelf. She opens cupboards, poking around, checking everything out.

Sitting on the couch, which converts into a double bed, I watch her intently, not saying a word as she openly snoops. The sun did a number on her today; her shoulders, her chest, even her nose is pink.

Eventually, she makes her way over to me, letting out a startled shriek when the boat rocks, before bursting out with laughter as she falls right into me, losing her balance. I grunt when her knee jabs into my side, and she giggles, grinning at me as she climbs onto my lap, straddling me.

Not what I anticipated her doing, but there's no goddamn way I'm going to complain about it.

Piper wraps her arms around me, cocking her head to the side, regarding me curiously. "I have no idea what I'm doing here. Why me? Why now after all this time?"

I don't respond to that because she doesn't give me a chance. All of a sudden, her mouth is on mine, and her hands, shaky and nervous, are tugging at the hem of my tee, pulling it up my chest.

"What are you doing?" I sound baffled because I am, but there's no way I'm going to stop her, not when her small, soft hands are brushing against my abs and sides invitingly.

She leans back at my question, though her hands don't still, yanking my shirt over my head. "I don't know. All I know is that I want you; I have for years and—" she gently grinds herself against my thickening cock, "I'm pretty sure you want me, too."

I nearly laugh. Of course I want her.

Been wanting her for years.

But, ah fuck me, if I can't get the damn words out, because her hands are sliding down my abs, fingertips dipping into the front of my jeans, working the button and zipper, and her lips are back on mine.

I should stop her. Make sure she's sure about this. She's had a few beers, and although I know she's not drunk, she's most likely still feeling a buzz.

But then her hand reaches between us, her fingertips smoothing over the tip of my cock, and fuck me, but I take it as an invitation.

An invitation to stop thinking.

My tongue darts out, stroking along the seam of her lips, and she willingly opens herself to me.

I kiss her deeply, single-mindedly, as my hands move from her hips to her ass, pulling her flush against me. She gasps, and then moans, digging her fingers into my hair and pressing herself closer still, grinding her core against my throbbing erection.

I groan at the pressure, rocking my hips up into her, my cock desperate for more.

More friction.

More pressure.

More of her.

I've never wanted to be inside a woman so much, or wanted to see a woman come as much as I do at this moment. I want to taste her, touch every inch of her body, feel her come on my hand, on my cock.

Piper breaks the kiss well before I'm ready and instant disappointment washes over me. She smirks at me, a one-sided lift of her lips, as she reaches up to the back of her neck and tugs the tie holding up her top.

I'm stunned speechless.

I watch the scant clothing fall, hanging around her middle, leaning back to stare at her as she reaches behind her back and pulls the second tie, letting her bikini top tumble to my lap.

Damn, she has nice tits. Round and perky, with tight pink nipples that are begging to be touched, licked, sucked on.

"We do this," I say, my voice a soft, near growl, "then you're in my bed and no one else's, yeah?"

She tenses at my words and a bright flush paints her cheeks. "Vance, please ..." she whimpers. "There's no other bed I want to be in. Just ... please ..."

Shit. I don't even know how to explain the elation that floods through me at hearing those words.

I grin at her. "Please what? Tell me what you want, freckles."

Piper growls at me—literally growls—and cocks an eyebrow, her expression equal parts nervous, frustrated, and challenging.

She's daring me to take over.

She's nervous that I will.

"Jesus, you're so damn pretty," I say, and though it nearly kills me, I ignore her perfect tits for a moment, leaning in and capturing her mouth once more.

Piper melts, the tension evaporates, and she kisses me back, frantic and needy.

It's ... awesome.

She's awesome.

Panting, her hands roam my skin, tug at my jeans, as I trace my tongue along her jaw, kissing down the column, along her shoulder, before dipping my head and capturing her pert nipple between my teeth, nipping and sucking at it.

"Vance," she moans, writhing on my lap. "Please."

"I got you, freckles."

I kiss along her collarbone as I move my hand between us. The warmth radiating from her core makes me shiver and she inhales sharply as I slip my fingers into her bikini bottom, groaning when I feel her arousal.

Piper dips her head, searching out my mouth and kissing me hard as I slide two fingers deep inside her.

"Oh, God ..." she gasps as I stroke my thumb over her clit

with each pump of my fingers. Within mere seconds, her body tightens, and her core flutters and squeezes against my digits buried inside her. She tilts her head back, arching her back and squeezing my shoulders as her orgasm rushes through her.

So damn pretty.

Piper lets her head fall to my shoulder, breathing hard as she kisses my neck. She squeaks out a high-pitched moan as I slowly remove my fingers from her center, shifting slightly, to dig out my wallet, looking for a condom. I pull it out, tossing the wallet beside us. It bounces off the couch, hitting the floor with a muted thud.

Lifting my hips, I fumble with my jeans and boxers, struggling to get them down and release my cock without letting her off my lap.

I want her where she is.

I want to watch her ride me.

I want her in control.

Pulling the strings at her hips, I tug the rest of her swimsuit away as she lifts up. She watches as I slide on the condom, her little pink tongue swiping along her bottom lip, and seconds later, she's lowering herself onto my dick.

The first thrust is slow and deep, and I groan at the sensation. She's so tight, so wet, I can barely contain myself, and it's a goddamn struggle to hold still and give her a moment to adjust.

Then she starts moving, slow and steady, her hands tightening on my shoulders, and I lose myself, thrusting up, picking up the rhythm, taking as much as I can.

I can feel it coming, building inside me. I reach between us, grazing my thumb over her clit. She lets out a shriek, squeezing me hard as her body convulses with pleasure, and I can't hold it back.

Shivering, I grunt into her mouth as I come, just as her orgasm starts to fade.

She doesn't move away, and I don't let her go, staying deep inside of her as I hold her against me. Her head drops back to my shoulder, her raspy breath blowing against my heated skin. I can feel her frantic pulse, the quick rise and fall of her chest, and I close my eyes, savoring the feeling of her skin against mine.

She's perfect, I think, squeezing her tightly. *Absolute perfection.*

Chapter Seventeen

Piper

"Where are you going?" Vance asks, his voice rougher, deeper than normal, as his hands grasp onto my hips and he pulls me back down beside him. I gasp in surprise, tumbling down onto the couch, and before I can respond, his mouth finds mine and he kisses me, slowly and thoroughly.

"I thought you were sleeping," I say when his mouth leaves mine, my voice no more than a whispered breath.

Sweeping my hair aside, he kisses the side of my neck, causing a shiver to spread through me. His lips trail along my neck and down my shoulder, pausing to place a kiss on the spot where they meet. His mouth lingers there as he whispers, "I'm awake."

"I see that," I say on a sigh, closing my eyes as he settles me back in his arms, maneuvering me to my side, pinning my back against his chest with no space separating our naked bodies.

It's late, well past nine at night, I assume. I'm not really sure. There are no clocks down here, but the sunset was at least an hour ago, and it feels like I've been lying here, wrapped up in Vance's arms, all sweaty and sticky, for hours.

They have been, hands down, the best hours of my life.

He chuckles in my ear as his hands caress my skin, slowly sliding down my belly, moving toward the dull ache between my legs. He trails a finger along my folds, before finding my clit, stroking and rubbing me, and it doesn't take long for my breaths to turn into whimpers.

"You didn't answer my question," he whispers. "Where were you going?"

"I thought …" My breath hitches, my voice strains as my body tightens, the pressure building up inside me. I take a sharp breath, releasing it on a whimper.

"You thought …" he prompts, his voice amused, and perhaps a little cocky.

He has stolen the words right from my lips.

"I thought I heard …" I try again, shifting my hips and pressing into his hand in a desperate search for more friction. I gasp when he circles the little bundle of nerves quicker and quicker, the rest of the words slipping from my lips, a disjointed mess of sounds. A moment later, my body tenses at the release of pleasure.

He hums in my ear, his hand stilling, cupping the place between my legs. "Love hearing the sounds you make when you come, freckles."

I'm embarrassed for a moment and my face begins to heat, but I don't have time to dwell on it, because he is suddenly on top of me, flipping me onto my back, his weight pressing down on me as he yanks my legs up around his waist.

My back arches involuntarily and I swallow a gasp as I feel his cock pressing against me, my eyes drifting closed as it brushes against my sensitive clit, sending small shocks of pleasure shooting through me.

"Open those eyes, Piper," he says quietly.

I do. My eyelids flutter open, my gaze locking on his. He grins down at me, kissing me quickly, before pulling back.

I make a sound of protest, lifting up as much as I can under the weight of his body, trying to reclaim his mouth, and he chuckles, shaking his head.

"Tell me," he says, "what was it you thought you heard?"

"What?" I ask, dazed.

"You heard something," he says, chuckling softly. "What was

it?"

Oh, right. "A phone ringing."

All at once, Vance slips away, climbing to his feet. Another sound of protest slips from my lips, but he doesn't pay attention to it, rummaging around on the floor, scooping up his pants and tugging them on.

He leaves without even looking back, and I lay there, staring at the steps leading above deck, not understanding what the heck just happened.

Mercifully, he isn't gone long so I don't have time to agonize over it. I don't even have time to consider getting dressed, because he returns after only a few seconds, slipping back down the steps soundlessly, haphazardly tossing my bag beside me on the couch, and he mutters that my phone was ringing too as he taps the screen on his and brings it to his ear.

Snagging my bag, I rifle through it, searching for my phone, listening to Vance's grunted curses as he listens to his messages.

Oh, crap.

Something's wrong.

I open my mouth but quickly close it, when my phone beeps with a new message. Not that I can say anything anyway. I'm too busy concentrating on not freaking out to speak.

I find my phone—finally—and I look at the screen. It's barely after ten, and several messages came through while I've been down here in the cabin, so I tap the screen and scroll through them.

Kim: Where are you?

Kim: Are you with Vance?

Kim: Why aren't you guys answering?

Jimmy: Pipes, I don't want to do this over text message. Call me. It's urgent.

Kim: This isn't the time to go silent on me.

Jimmy: What the hell is the point of having a fucking cell phone if you're not going to answer it?

Kim: Please, please, please call me.

Jimmy: I swear to God, if you guys don't call us back right now ...

Kim: You need to call me back. RIGHT. NOW.

I stare at the screen, blinking at the last message, feeling my stomach coil tight as I drop the phone onto the couch beside me, and glance at Vance. His back is to me, and he's whispering now, talking to someone on the phone. I don't know who he's talking to or what he's talking about; his responses are all short and hissed—one-word answers.

The conversation doesn't last long, only a few short seconds before he ends the call, and as he turns to me, I suddenly feel exposed and very naked.

"What's wrong?" I whisper as I stand up, and move across the small area to my dress, quickly slipping it on.

He blinks at me when I look back at him, and I bite down on my bottom lip, growing more and more concerned when he doesn't respond right away, my anxiety making me feel sick.

Years pass, it seems, before Vance speaks.

"There's a problem at your house," he says quietly, watching me closely.

I feel my whole body tense and coil with a mix of anxiety and dread. What happened now? Oh God, is this ever going to end?

"What kind of problem?" My voice is shaky and hesitant, and my stomach and chest squeeze tight.

Vance's eyes darken at my question. He hears my panic. He sees it.

"Shit," he mutters, scrubbing a hand over his face. "Shit, I shouldn't have brought ..." he trails off, mumbling a fresh array of curses.

His hand drops from his face and my stomach coils nervously.

"Your house ..." he continues, and then stalls, hesitating for a moment. "Piper, honey, your house is on fire."

I look up at him and a shocked laugh rocks from me. My house is on fire. I have no idea what he means by that, or perhaps it's just my brain refusing to understand his words, but his tone tells me it's not a little kitchen mishap, or a knocked over candle.

Oh my God.

My house is on fire.

"Jimmy ..."

"No one was there," he says quickly, before I can finish my thought. "Jimmy was out with his girl when the fire started."

"Was this ...? Is this ...?" I stall. I don't even know what I'm trying to ask as I back up a step.

Squeezing my eyes shut, I continue to back up away from him until my calves hit the couch, and I fall down onto it. A sob breaks free from my chest, a mix of distress and relief battling through my system, and he moves to me, crouching down and reaching forward, pulling me to his chest. I close my eyes and press my forehead against his shoulder, and I cry.

"Freckles," he says, the uneasiness seeping into his tone making my heart squeeze. "Honey, don't cry. Firefighters are already there, so is Jase and Wes, Jimmy and Kim. It's gonna be okay."

Sniffling loudly, I pull away from him, wiping my face with the palms of my hands. "We have to go. I need to get home."

"You just stay down here, yeah?" he says, placing a comforting hand on my shoulder, holding me still as I try to rise. "I'll get us back to the docks as quickly as I can."

I want to help him get us back, but I can't. I don't know how, don't have a clue what to do, so I do as he says, staying put on the couch, knowing I'll just be in the way if I try to follow him.

My knees shake as I fidget with my dress, chewing on my bottom lip, as the boat speeds back to the docks. It feels as though it takes hours for us to stop, and another hour for Vance to secure the boat and round up our things, before we're finally piling into his truck.

Vance pulls out of the parking lot and speeds until we reach my house. We don't speak on the drive, but he does keep a comforting hand on my thigh the entire way, rubbing and squeezing, trying to ease my nervousness. I spend the drive with my focus on the dashboard, trying hard to keep my cool and not hyperventilate.

He parks at the curb, behind a line of police cruisers, and I'm out of the truck, walking toward the chaos before he even cuts the engine.

It feels strange walking toward my house right now.

Unreal.

It's too bright, too many lights flashing and people shouting. My neighbors are lining the sidewalk, trying to get a look.

Strange and overwhelming.

Vance comes up behind me as I reach the fire truck, his large, warm hand wrapping gently around my bicep, pulling me to a stop. The truck is parked half on my lawn and half on the street, blocking all traffic, the hose hooked up to the fire hydrant at the curb in front of my neighbor's house.

"Piper, hold up a second," he says. "You can't just run in there, honey."

"Right," I whisper, my head bobbing up and down. "We should find the person in charge and, uh, maybe—"

"Yo, Vance!" someone shouts, and my words stall as I turn to see Wes jogging toward us, Kim struggling to keep up behind him.

Vance squeezes my bicep, his warm hand reassuring and comforting, and then he lets go, turning his full attention to Wes, as he launches in, giving us all the details.

I hear words like firebomb … kitchen … living room … through the windows … contained … partial from the cameras … red Mustang … license plate … but my brain doesn't register the entire conversation, as my eyes take in the firefighters and police and the smoke still coming from my house.

So many people.

So much smoke.

And then my eyes land on my truck, parked in the driveway.

"How did my truck get here?" I ask, interrupting Wes, frowning with confusion.

Vance cuts his dark eyes to mine. "What?"

"My truck," I say. "How did it get here?"

His brow furrows and he regards me peculiarly, as though he's not sure why I'm worrying about my truck right now. "Jase picked it up from the shop and brought it over this afternoon."

Feeling a chill that has nothing to do with the cool night air, I wrap my arms around myself, shivering. "Do you think the person thought I was home?"

"Piper," Kim whispers, her gaze holding steady on my distraught face as she grabs my hand, squeezing it. "Aw, sweetie, don't think about that. It's going to be okay."

I blink at her. Don't think about it? How can I possibly not think about it?

Vance's arm comes around me then, pulling me tight into his side. My body is trembling, I realize. I can feel it vibrating against his arm. I feel my stomach turn and my heart race.

Oh God, I think I'm going to be sick.

I say nothing, because I don't know what to say. My gaze shifts back to my house, my eyes taking in the smoke pouring out of the broken windows and the firefighters moving in and out of the doorway, making sure the fire is out.

I'm aware that Vance and Wes are still talking, but I don't have a clue what's being said.

This is bad.

I thought it was bad before. My God, I was in a car accident because of this … this person, but this …

"Plates belong to Tara Smith," Jase says as he walks over to us, drawing my attention away from my house. "Cruz is sending a unit to her place now."

Chapter Eighteen

Vance

"Hey."

I pull my eyes away from my cell phone and look up as Piper slides onto the couch beside me. I blink a few times, trying to clear the image of the text message I just received from my mind, but it does little to help. The damn message has imprinted itself behind my eyes, twisting up my insides and leaving a sour taste in my mouth.

I glance at her, forcing a smile, and then I do a double take when I notice she's wearing one of my old tees. It's large on her, hanging off one shoulder and falling mid-thigh, but she looks good in it.

Really good.

"Hey," I say quietly, my smile suddenly feeling more genuine as I turn to face her. "How you doing, freckles?"

"I'm okay," she replies just as quietly, eyeing me strangely. "You look, uh ... tense. Is something wrong?"

I stare at her, surprised she picked up on my unease. I'm usually pretty good at hiding my emotions and keeping my expression blank.

I don't respond right away, my eyes instinctively gliding along her face and over her body, wondering if she really is okay. It's shortly after nine in the morning, and we're at my apartment. We woke up about twenty minutes ago, and the first thing Piper did was pick up her phone and call the insurance company, which I'm sure wasn't fun.

But as my eyes trail over her, I notice that she looks okay. Tired and a little stressed, but there's a subtle determination in her eyes that tells me she's holding it together.

"It's not my truck, is it?" she asks, her tone slightly panicked. "Please don't tell me something's wrong with my baby. I just got it back."

I smirk, letting out an amused laugh. Of course she'd worry about her truck. "It's not your truck, freckles."

"Then what is it?" she asks, looking skeptical.

I cut my eyes to my phone, still clasped in my hand, before glancing back at her. Might as well get it over and done with, I guess. "You want the good news or the bad news first?"

I see her flinch at my words and she pulls her feet up onto the couch, hugging her knees to her chest, leaning away from me. She looks at me, her eyes cagey, and she whispers, "There's bad news?"

Shit.

Shit, shit, shit.

I've seen that look before on her and I don't like it.

Not one bit.

It's a look she's given me a hundred times before, the one that comes just before she runs away, or dismisses me, and seeing it right now cuts deep.

Really fucking deep.

Maybe it isn't the same one. It's possible she's just feeling overwhelmed by the shit storm surrounding her, but it sure feels like she's about to blow me off.

I reach over, putting my hand on her cheek. A nervous tick there has all of my protective instincts firing up. I want to take care of her—more so than usual—and the sudden worry that she isn't going to let me has my nerves on edge.

Moving my hand from her cheek, I settle it at the nape of her neck, squeezing gently. "Yeah, Piper, there's bad news."

Sucking in a breath, she closes her eyes, and turns her face away, considering for a tick. "I suppose I should go with the bad news first, but I don't think I want to hear it. Ever. Maybe you can just give me the good news and keep the bad to yourself?"

Her response makes me chuckle, and she gives me a dirty look, pursing her lips, and I let my hand drop from her neck. "Thought you wanted to be informed and involved."

"Yeah, well, I think I want to change my mind on that," she says. "At least for today."

"Okay, freckles," I say, chuckling again. "Good news it is then. Cruz pulled in Chad Miller last night and he ID'd Tara as the blonde who paid him to loosen your tire."

She frowns and tugs her bottom lip between her teeth, biting on it. "Okay ... Okay. That's good, I think, for Chad at least. So, what's the bad news?"

I cock a brow at her. "Thought you didn't want to know the bad news."

She shrugs a shoulder. "Well, I want to know it now."

She sounds not nearly as confident as normal, and I hesitate, knowing she's not going to like what I have to tell her, but I can feel her gaze as she waits for my response as I set my cell phone down on the coffee table, and pick up my coffee, taking a deep sip.

"They haven't found Tara yet," I say slowly, keeping my tone as unbothered by the news as possible. "Cops searched her place and by the looks of things, they're figuring she took off in a rush. Clothes were a mess, all over the bedroom, and her dresser drawers were half emptied, hanging open. They've put out a BOLO on both her and her car, but so far, nothing."

"You've got to be kidding me," she mutters under her breath, and then she scrunches up her nose, looking at me curiously. "Uh, what's a BOLO?"

"It means be on the look-out," I tell her, and take another sip of my coffee. "I also heard from Jimmy while you were on the phone with the insurance company. Tara reached out to him. Sent him a text saying she was going to her parents in Orlando. She needs time to think about the baby. Cruz has that information, too, and he's working on setting up a unit on that end to pick her up when she arrives."

"This is really screwed up," she says. "All of it. I just ... I don't even know what to think. The spray paint ... the warnings ... She wants me to stay away from Jimmy, but I don't understand how she could think that there's anything going on between us."

I do. At first I thought the same thing. The two of them are close. Too close. And even though I know they are just friends, and that they work together, it's been hell knowing that he's living with her.

Pure hell.

I can completely see how Jimmy's ex would think that there was more going on between them than there is.

But instead of getting into that, I say, "You didn't tell me Jimmy's ex is knocked up."

"It wasn't my news to tell," she says, shrugging a shoulder. "And she's not really pregnant. According to Jimmy, she can't have kids. It's just a story, something to get his attention, something to guilt him into coming back."

I'm silent for a moment, regarding her incredulously. She says it as though it's no big deal, and to her, perhaps it isn't. To me, though ... If I'd have known that Jimmy's ex was causing him so much trouble, I would have looked into her already. Might have even been able to stop this shit before it went this far. She hadn't put either of them on the secondary list I had her write up. Never mentioned a word about his issues. But I can tell by looking at her that she never thought about it, never considered the fact that all the vandalism could have been because of one of her friends, so I don't push it.

There's no point, and it'll probably just piss her off.

"How'd it go with the insurance company?" I ask casually, shifting the topic. "You get everything settled there?"

She hesitates, narrowing her eyes at me, and for a long moment, I think she's going to ask more questions about Tara. Questions I just don't have the answers to—yet.

"I'm not really sure," she replies eventually. "They're sending an adjuster over to my house for eleven, so I guess I'll know more after that."

"We'll head over there after I get some food in you," I say. "Want you to pack up whatever you're gonna need to stay here for the next little while."

"Oh, uh, thanks, but you don't have to take me. Kim's meeting me there and ..." she stalls for a tick, her brow furrowing, as she regards me hesitantly. "Did you just say I'm staying here for the, uh, next little while?"

I nod. "Yeah, I did."

"I can't do that," she says right away, shaking her head.

I cock a brow at her. "Why the fuck not?"

"Because, I, uh ..." Her face flushes. "I ... I just don't think that's a good idea."

My brow dips as I frown at her. "You're my girl and I take care of what's mine, so I'm not seeing what isn't good about you staying here."

"I'm your girl?" she asks. Her tone is hesitant, but a small smile touches her lips and her pretty eyes brighten with both fear and excitement.

I nod my head slowly, grinning as I watch her head bob up and down with mine.

So goddamn adorable.

"I've got a feeling you've been my girl for a long time now," I say, inching toward her slowly, my expression serious. "I was just too stupid to realize it."

Piper's eyes sparkle and her cheeks burn brighter. She tugs the corner of her bottom lip between her teeth, biting it nervously. "I ... uh ... I ..."

"You get that I'm keeping you, right?" I ask, ignoring her stammers, staring her in the eyes as I move closer still, until the tip of my nose brushes against hers.

Her breath hitches, but she doesn't move away, instead, leaning into me and pressing a barely there kiss on my lips. "Good," she whispers against my mouth. "Because I think I want to keep you, too."

Piper

"Are you sure you want to do this?" Kim sounds nervous and she clearly isn't all that thrilled that I've chosen to stay with Vance instead of moving back into my room at her place. She's sitting on Vance's bed, legs crossed and elbows on her knees, watching me as I unpack the few things I managed to grab from my house.

"Yes, I'm sure," I say as I grab one of my tops, sniff it, and toss it back in my bag. The fire was contained to the living room and kitchen, but the scent of smoke wasn't and it's clinging to most of the fabric.

"I just don't understand why you won't come back to the apartment," she says exasperatedly. "Your room's still there, exactly how you left it."

I let out a sharp laugh. "So it's completely empty?"

"No," she says. "It still has that bookcase in it."

"Kim, that bookcase isn't mine and it's built into the wall. Of course it's still there."

She frowns at me and raises an eyebrow, silently asking me if I have a point.

Sighing, I pick up a pair of skinny jeans and give them a sniff. *Ugh, smoky.* I should probably just dump everything into the wash and be done with it, but I'm really hoping to find something—anything—clean enough to wear tonight for Jason's barbeque.

"He cleaned out a drawer and half the closet for you."

"So ...?"

Kim rolls her eyes, a slight flush pinking her cheeks as she rolls onto her stomach on the bed, and stares at me with her chin in her hands. "So ... that means he's serious. I don't think you're ready for his kind of serious."

Tell me about it.

No, scratch that, don't tell me. My nerves are jumpy enough as it is.

I cut my eyes at her. "I don't understand why you suddenly have such an issue with me hooking up with Vance."

"Piper," she stalls, sighing dramatically. "I don't have an issue with you and Vance. I'm happy about it. Honestly happy. It's just that … It's just that I want to make sure you're doing this for you, because you want to be here with him, and not because Vance bossed you into it."

I give her a bored look, hoping it'll mask my own nerves as I try to calm them. The truth is, Vance did sort of boss me into staying with him, but I also didn't protest too much, because when a badass hottie asks you to stay with him, you consider it, but when a badass hottie asks you to stay with him and then tells you you're his girl, you do it. No questions asked.

"I want to be here," I say. "I trust him and I think it's safer for all of us if I'm staying here."

Rolling her eyes, she gives me a look. "Where is he, anyway? He didn't even say goodbye to me before taking off from your place. He never does that."

I shrug. "He got a call from Wes, but he should be here soon." Then, needing a shift in topic, I ask, "Have you heard from Jimmy today?"

"Yeah, he got a room at Clear River Inn. I told him he could stay with me, but with Tara being MIA and the fire at your place …" she lets her words fall off, shrugging helplessly.

My brow furrows. I'm not sure how to feel about that. "He won't answer my calls. All I got was a text message that said I'm sorry."

"Well, he should be." I'm momentarily caught off guard by her sharp response, and before I can question her anymore, her phone chimes. Kim jumps up off the bed, darting across the room to her purse, and rummages through it. She pulls out her phone, glances at it, and then groans. "Crap, I've gotta run. Stupid dentist appointment. I'll give you a call later, and remember, the room's there for you if you want it, okay?"

"Okay," I reply. "I'll remember that."

With a quick hug, she's out of the room and rushing for the door, her purse slung over her shoulder. To be honest, I don't expect to think about my old room at all.

Once she's gone, I flip the deadbolt back in place and then

head to the kitchen to check on the pie. I open the oven, glance in, and then shut it again. It could still use another couple of minutes, I think.

I pull out my phone, and send Jimmy another *please call me back* message, before puttering around the kitchen, cleaning up and washing a few dishes.

I'm just about to take the pie out when the door opens, and I glance over to see Vance coming in.

"Hey," I say, offering him a smile as I open the oven, and grabbing a couple of towels, I pull the pie out, setting it down to cool on the stovetop.

Vance comes over to me, and wraps an arm around my neck as I close the oven, turning me to him and leaning in for a long wet kiss that tastes of coffee and a sweetness that's entirely him. My arms come up, wrapping around his neck as his hands trail down my sides, cupping my bottom, and I let out a surprised shriek as he lifts me up, setting me on the countertop. He nudges at my knees, pushing my legs open, and moves his big body between them.

When I'm settled where he wants me, Vance pulls away and cradles my face in his hands. "Hey, freckles," he says, smiling down at me. "Is there any particular reason the apartment smells like smoke?"

"I brought some clothes back from my house and I, uh, also kind of burnt a pie."

His gaze shifts from my face to the pie, and his brow bunches. "It doesn't look burnt to me."

"That's the second try," I say, blushing. "The first one came out black."

Vance brings his eyes back to me, regarding me curiously. "Any particular reason you're baking a pie?"

I nod slowly. "Yes."

He cocks an eyebrow at me. "You gonna share that reason?"

"Well, I was going to bake a cake, but the meeting with the insurance adjuster took longer than I thought it would and I knew I wouldn't have enough time for it to cool before putting on the icing. Then I remembered that you like apple pie, so I stopped by the grocery store and picked up the stuff to make one and got it in the oven, but then Kim showed up and I forgot to set the timer and I burnt it, so I started again."

A legitimate look of surprise mixed with confusion crosses his face, and my cheeks heat with embarrassment. Oh, God. What's wrong with me? I'm rambling, babbling on to him about cakes and pies without taking a breath.

"Freckles, why are you baking anything at all?" he asks, curiously.

"Because this is Elena's welcome home party," I say. "And you need home baked stuff for welcome home parties."

He laughs, genuinely amused. "Have I told you how adorable you are?"

I shake my head, grinning at him. "Nope, not yet."

He laughs again, shaking his head. "You're adorable." He kisses me again, this time, just a quick press of his lips to mine, before stepping away from me. "Go grab whatever you need, yeah? We've gotta get going."

Slipping off the countertop, I grab my things, sticking my phone in my bag before wrapping the pie in a towel, and careful not to burn myself, I follow Vance out the door. Jase's place is only about a ten-minute drive away. It's hot outside, the air stifling from the late afternoon sun. It doesn't seem to faze Vance, but I crank up the air-conditioner as soon as he starts up the truck.

Vance rambles on about Elena the entire drive. She's shy, she's sweet, she's loyal. He tells me she's completely in love with Jase, that Jase hasn't been the same without her here. There's respect in his voice when he speaks of her, respect and emotion. It's pretty obvious he thinks highly of her, and cares about her a lot.

When we arrive at Jase's place, Wes is standing in the street, leaning against his car. He pushes off the car as we park, shoving his hands in the pockets of his jeans. He's grinning— Wes always seems to be grinning about something—and he takes a couple steps toward us as we hop out of the vehicle.

"Yo," he says, lifting his chin. "Any chance you brought your keys?"

Vance laughs. "Jase is gonna shoot you if you lost the keys to his house again."

"I didn't lose them," Wes says, smiling sheepishly. "They're in a safe place; I just don't remember exactly where that place is at the moment."

Vance chuckles, casting an amused look at him as he makes his way up the driveway, keys in hand. I stroll along behind, letting him take the lead as he unlocks the front door, and moves into the house.

It's quiet inside. Really quiet. And if it weren't for Jase's car and what I assume is Elena's new truck in the driveway, I would think no one is home.

Wes follows us in and pauses, regarding me strangely for a moment, before his eyes cut to the pie I'm holding. His brows lift up in shock. "You made a pie?"

I nod, flushing slightly. "Um, yeah."

"That's fuckin' awesome," he says. "I love pie."

Vance laughs, and Wes's grin widens as he purposefully slams the door behind him, and then bolts for the stairs. His footsteps are loud, thundering down the hallway, and then I hear him bang on a door and shout, "Yo, Elena! Jase! Get your asses dressed and downstairs. It's barbeque time."

"Oh my God, did he just, uh, interrupt them?" I ask, unable to help myself. I keep my voice low, though, hoping no one will overhear me.

"Yep," Vance says, taking the pie from my hands, and walking toward what I assume is the kitchen.

I follow him, shaking my head. *Awkward.* "That's so not cool."

My response makes him laugh, and he glances over his shoulder. "She loves barbeques. She ain't gonna care."

I gape at him. I'm pretty sure he's wrong on that. "I hope you're right."

"I am," he says, smirking, as he enters the kitchen. He sets the pie down, and goes straight for the fridge, pulling it open and retrieving two beers, before closing it and strolling over to me, handing me one. "Come on, let's go out back."

He doesn't wait for me to respond, dropping an arm over my shoulder, and guiding me toward the patio doors. We go outside, and Vance ushers me over to the barbeque, and gets to work starting it up.

Moments later, Wes joins us. He starts talking to Vance about a new case, something about a divorce and a dog, though I'm not really listening. I'm too busy glancing around the yard, my gaze wandering over the insanely large padlock on the gate leading to the front, and all the motion sensors scattered around the yard. The security measures seem overboard to me, and I nearly laugh. Looks like Vance isn't the only security system enthusiast in the bunch.

My gaze continues to wander over the large deck and patio set, stalling when it hits the doors, and I spot Jase, standing with a woman just inside. She's cute, and slightly shorter than me, with dark brown hair, blonde roots, and bright blue eyes. She stands at the door, hesitating for a moment. Jase says something to her, and she quickly shakes her head. Her smile is shaky, and so is her hand as she reaches for the patio door.

I turn to Vance, about to ask him if she's okay, but he's already on the move, climbing the steps to the deck. He wraps Elena in a hug at the same time as Wes, squeezing her so tightly it looks painful.

I hang back and watch them, my heart pounding in my chest. I feel a little out of my comfort zone and completely out of place watching them.

The four of them seem so ... close. So comfortable with each other.

I almost feel like an intruder watching a precious moment between friends.

No, not friends.

Family.

Jase is smiling, and his eyes are smiling, too, as he watches the three of them. He looks younger somehow, more relaxed than I've ever seen him before, and I'm guessing it's because of her.

He loves her.

A lot.

It radiates from him, pours off him.

Elena laughs. It's a beautiful sound. Not too high, not too loud, as Jase mutters, "Jesus, let her go. You idiots are gonna suffocate her."

Vance and Wes let her go, and I laugh when I hear them grumbling something about Jase hogging her as they do.

"You ain't allowed to leave for four weeks again," Vance says seriously. "Not unless you take him with you. Can't handle the fuckin' moping."

"Shut up," Jase says.

Wes laughs. "He barely slept."

"Shut up," Jase repeats, louder.

"He wouldn't go to the bar with us because he didn't want to miss a call with you," Vance continues, grinning like a fool.

Jason's arms come around Elena's waist, pulling her to his side, and he groans and mutters, "Shut the fuck up."

Elena laughs, tilting her head, looking up at him. He watches her, brow cocked as though daring her to say something, but she doesn't. She just laughs and hugs him back.

"Yo, Piper," Wes says after a moment. "Come over here, babe."

At the sound of my name, my heart somehow pounds a little harder, and my feet start to move. Slowly, I climb the steps, moving over to the group as Elena unwinds herself from Jase.

"This is Piper," Wes says, waving a hand toward me. "Piper, meet Elena."

I smile, offering a little wave. "Good to meet you. I've heard so much about you."

Elena lets out a groan at my words. "Whatever they said, don't believe them. These guys are the best liars I've ever met."

I laugh softly, not doubting it for a second. The three of them have mastered the blank face expression. "It was all good. I swear."

The guys laugh at us, and Vance grins and winks at me, before making his way over to the barbeque with Wes and Jase.

They joke around, laughing and carrying on like a bunch of teenagers, while Elena and I sit on the deck.

Neither of us talk much. I'm not really sure what to say, and she seems content enough to just watch the guys as they laugh.

I get lost in my own head, mulling over what to do about my house. My computer and everything in my office came out unscathed—thank God, but I'm going to need to pick out new furniture, and basically an entire new kitchen. The fire ate away at my cupboards and counters, leaving not much more than the ruined remains of the appliances. The living room furniture was all destroyed, too, and the walls need repair and paint. If I want to change the colors or decor, now is the time to do it, I guess, though I doubt I will.

I loved my house.

Everything about it.

Late afternoon morphs into early evening. We eat and drink and laugh, and I relax, slowly beginning to feel like a part of their group, and start having a good time.

No. Scratch that. I'm having a fantastic time.

After we finish eating, Vance leans into me, telling me he'll be right back, before he gets up and heads into the house. He strolls back out moments later, carrying a guitar. His eyes cut to me, and I raise an eyebrow in question as he takes a seat on the steps, but he merely smirks.

And then he starts to play.

And he's good.

Really good.

It takes me a moment to recognize the song, but when I do, I freeze and I feel my jaw go slack. It's the song ... the one from the bar ... the one from the truck ...

How did he learn it so quickly?

No, wait ... why did he even want to learn it?

My stomach flutters, the butterflies soaring within me as I listen to the music.

I don't want to think about what it means.

I don't want to believe it could mean anything.

But I hope, oh God do I hope, it means something.

Something wonderful.

The silence that follows the last cord snaps me out of my frozen state.

"Oh my God," I whisper, setting my beer down. I jump up from my chair and sprint across the deck to where Vance sits on the steps.

He looks up at me, a big shit-eating grin spread on his lips. "Hey, Piper."

"Play it again," I blurt. "That was amazing. Please, play it again."

Vance barks out a laugh, his eyes twinkling with satisfaction. I'm vaguely aware of the others talking, and I hardly notice Wes's chuckles in the background, because Vance does what I ask.

He plays it again.

And it's amazing.

Chapter Nineteen

Vance

"Vance, have you seen my ..."

Piper darts into the kitchen, her gaze searching the room, her words stalling. She looks frazzled this morning, and out of sorts. She's been rushing around for the last thirty minutes, getting ready to leave.

It's curious.

Curious and slightly unnerving.

I'm sitting at the kitchen table, sipping my coffee, watching her questioningly, but just like the last time she ran in here, and the time before that, she doesn't notice. I don't bother asking what she's looking for, knowing she's not really expecting an answer from me. I've heard that question at least half a dozen times since breakfast and I gave up trying to help after the third.

"There it is," she grumbles and rushes over to the counter, scooping up a tube of lip balm and muttering something under her breath, before rushing back out of the room.

She's seems so nervous and I wonder if it's because she's seeing Jimmy for the first time since the fire or if it's that she's going to see him alone.

Neither scenario sits well with me.

It's been a week and a half, give or take a day, with no contact from Tara. There has been no spray painting, no notes, no threats, no text message or phone calls to Jimmy, just a whole lot of silence.

Day after day, Piper habitually goes to her house. She claims it's only to check out the construction progress, but I think she's secretly expecting to find some clue that Tara is still in the city.

It's been ... weird having her here. Weird in an awesome sort of way.

I'm not going to lie, there's been a few times over the last week that I've freaked out a little. Things are just so easy with her. So comfortable, and it's left me feeling out of sorts.

I feel like I just met her.

I feel like I've known her forever.

It's ... confusing and it's amazing.

Piper rushes back into the kitchen, her lips pursed as she starts scanning the counters again. Her hair is now in a loose braid, the tail of it hanging over one shoulder, and she's changed her clothing for what must be the tenth time this morning, now wearing a pair of deep blue boot cut jeans, and a basic white ribbed tank.

She stalls near me, just out of reach, and makes a disgruntled noise from the back of her throat, finally looking at me. "Vance, where did you put my—"

"Come here, freckles," I say, interrupting her, pushing away from the table and holding out my hand to her. "Wanna talk to you for a second."

She frowns at me, hesitating. She looks as though she's about to protest, but as I flick my finger at her, beckoning for her to come to me, her hesitation melts away and she smirks, shaking her head.

Piper moves across the short space, and as soon as she's in reaching distance, I pull her to me, maneuvering her between my legs, cupping her hip with one hand and her ass with the other. She makes a startled sound at my abrupt movement as she teeters on her feet, and then she giggles, bringing her hands up to my shoulders, steadying herself.

I tilt my face up to look at her. She looks worried, so I offer her a smile to try to ease her concern, and ask, "What's going on with you this morning?"

She returns my smile timidly, cocking her head to the side as she shrugs a shoulder. "Nothing's going on. Why would you think something is going on?"

Sighing, I relax back in the chair, pulling her closer, relishing the feel of her pressed against me. "You're scattered and that's the tenth outfit and hairstyle you've tried in the last thirty minutes."

Pink colors her cheeks, and she dips her chin down, her eyes falling from mine. "You noticed that, huh?"

"Yeah, freckles, I noticed." I stare at her for a tick, and then lift a questioning eyebrow. "Did you tell Jimmy you're coming to help?"

I'm not sure why I bother asking her the question. I already know the answer. She wouldn't be this nervous or this scattered if she had told him.

She shakes her head, confirming it. "No. He's still not returning my calls or messages, so I thought ..." she stalls, scrunching her nose up. "I thought maybe I should just show up and force him to talk to me. Kim says he's still blaming himself and it's not his fault. I need to fix this."

I nod, not surprised. He's kept me updated, though only through text messages, and any time I've broached the topic of him talking to Piper, he simply ignores me.

"I'll come with you if you want," I say. "I can shift my meeting around."

She blows out a dismissive breath, her eyes darting back to mine. "No, no, you don't have to do that. It's fine."

"I know I don't have to," I say, "but I will if you want me to."

She laughs, casting me an amused look as she shakes her head. "No, really, you don't have to. Kim is going to be there around one and I really want to have some time with just him. I miss him, you know?"

"Yeah, I get it," I say. "You change your mind, though, you call me, yeah?"

She nods and I expect her to try to move away, knowing

she's in a hurry, but she doesn't. Instead, she wiggles around in my grip, shifting until she's able to sit on my lap. She looks up at me, her arm wrapped around my shoulder, and smiles genuinely. "You're pretty awesome."

I chuckle, kissing her lips. "You're pretty awesome, too."

Piper

Jimmy's new apartment building isn't old, and it isn't exactly ... new. It's somewhere in that middle stage where it could use a little sprucing up, but still looks good as it is.

I pull into the lot, and park my truck in one of the visitor spaces, spotting Jimmy's white Honda parked by the building's main doors. The trunk is open, so is the rear passenger side door, but Jimmy is nowhere in sight.

Reaching into my purse, I grab my cell and search for the text message Kim sent me to double check the apartment number. It takes a moment to find it; my nerves are so rattled that I must skim past it a few times before it finally catches my eye.

Fifth floor, apartment 521.

I put my phone back in my purse, and glance at the building once more. My hands begin to sweat, and my stomach coils tight. What if he doesn't listen to me? What if he doesn't believe me?

Crap, maybe I should have brought Vance with me.

Better yet, I should have waited for Kim.

Ugh. That sounds ridiculous.

Jimmy's been a friend of mine for years. We've worked together. We've lived together. We've been through so much together ...

Okay, right, stop worrying.

Get out of the truck, Pipes, and fix this.

I hop out of the truck, quickly making my way to the main doors, pausing for just a second to snag a box of dishes from the open trunk of Jimmy's car. Might as well bring something up while I'm going, right?

The elevator is quick, already waiting at the lobby. I get in and push the button, and moments later it opens right outside Jimmy's apartment door. I stroll up to the door, juggling the box around, knocking.

Then I wait.

And wait.

And wait some more.

I can hear him in there, crashing around, unpacking and making a heck of a lot of noise doing it. There's music playing, too, so I knock again, this time louder.

The door opens and he appears in front of me, his expression confused. He looks at me, his eyes shifting past me for just a second, scanning the empty hallway at my back, before he meets my eyes again. He's quiet for a moment, just staring at me, agitatedly pulling his lip ring between his teeth, worrying it, before he finally speaks. "Pipes."

That's it.

That's all he says.

"Hey, Jimmy," I say, smiling at him.

He stares at me. "What are you doing here?"

I shrug my shoulder awkwardly, rearranging the box in my hands. Jesus, it's getting heavy. "I thought maybe you could use some help."

He blinks, then stares some more, his expression shifting from confusion to ... I don't even know. Angry? Annoyed? Depressed?

It could be anything really.

The silence stretches.

"Uh ..." I stall, hesitating. Maybe this just showing up idea wasn't such a good plan after all. "This box is kind of heavy."

Jimmy's eyes widen, dropping from mine to the box clutched in my arms, as though he's only now just noticing it. He reaches for it, taking it from my hands, and quickly sets it down in the hallway.

"Fuck, Pipes ..." he mutters, turning back to me. "Fuck, I'm so sorry."

Suddenly, he's on me, arms wrapped around me, hugging me so tightly I can hardly pull in a breath, but I don't care. I hug him back, my arms coming around his waist, squeezing just as tightly.

"You have nothing to be sorry for," I say softly but firmly, my voice muffled by his chest. Pulling my head back, I grin up at him. "Well, maybe you need to be a little sorry, because I've been going out of my mind worrying about you, but that's it."

"Tara ..." he starts, but I don't let him finish, pushing out of his arms.

"Tara has nothing to do with you and me," I say. "It's not your fault she was harassing me."

His eyes are skeptical, borderline angry as he takes a step back. He doesn't believe me.

"I'm serious, Jimmy," I say. "This crap that's happened to me is not your fault."

His eyebrows furrow at my statement. "But ..."

"No," I say, cutting him off once more. "No buts. This is not your fault and Tara is not your problem. She can't hide forever. Vance will find her, or the cops will, and when they do, she'll have to deal with the consequences. Not you. You can't blame yourself for her obsession."

He gapes at me. "You really don't blame me?"

I shake my head. "No, I really don't blame you."

He stares at the floor for a moment, before meeting my eyes, returning my smile. I don't know if he believes me, but I can tell he wants to.

"You left your car door and trunk open," I tell him. "That's probably not smart."

"Probably not," he agrees.

"Should we ...?" I hesitate, looking past him to the disaster of boxes spread through the apartment, then back to the elevator. "Can I ...?"

I'm not sure why I can't spit the questions out, but the words just won't come. He looks exhausted and stressed, and standing at the door, I feel like I'm interfering.

"Yeah, Pipes," he says, answering my unasked questions. "I

think I'd like that."

He strolls out the door, a smile tugging at his lips as he moves past me, pressing the call button on the elevator, and we head back down to his car, making quick work of unloading the rest of the boxes.

The morning slips by as we unpack. Nearly everything is new, still in the original packaging. New clothes, new sheets, new pillows and dishes. When I ask him about it, he grumbles something about Tara tossing all his things while he was away on his last photo shoot, before taking off to another room, clearly not wanting to talk about it.

By the time we finish unpacking everything for the bedroom and setting it up with the new bed and dresser, it's closing in on one o'clock.

"I'm starving," Jimmy says, flopping back on his bed. "You feel like pizza?"

I look at him, my expression serious. "I always feel like pizza."

"There's a place down a block that's awesome and they have a walk in special running," he says. "You wanna come?"

"Kim's going to be here any minute," I remind him. "One of us should probably stick around."

Sitting up, he runs a hand over his face. "Yeah, okay. Pineapple and bacon, right? Or did you want to go instead?"

"Nah, I'll stick around here," I say, though I'm guessing he wasn't expecting me to want to go, because he's already up and walking toward the door.

I spend some time in the kitchen after he leaves, washing all the new dishes, and then I wander between rooms for a bit, putting things away.

There's a knock on the door as I bend over to grab a box labeled bathroom. I straighten up, leaving the box where it is, and glance at the clock, seeing it's a few minutes after one. I smile. Kim's actually on time. I walk to the door, quickly unlocking it, and pull it open, but it's not Kim on the other side of the door.

No, the person standing at the door is Tara.

Chapter Twenty

Piper

Oh crap!

Oh crap!

Oh crap!

My pulse goes flying and I move to push the door closed, but before I can, hard hands shove me and I stumble backward. I gasp in shock, nearly toppling over, scrambling to stay on my feet as the door slams and the lock clicks in place.

I try to swallow my shriek as Tara spins on me, but the sound leaks out as a high-pitched gargling mess when she takes a threatening step in my direction. She's a mess. Her clothes, stained and torn, her hair, tangled and greasy, and her eyes ... oh God, her eyes are crazy and wild, and she has a grin on her face that terrifies me. It's twisted and wrong, making her look deranged and almost feral.

She stalks toward me, muttering incoherent words, and I scramble backwards, my hands up in front of me, warding her off.

"What are you doing here?" I ask, hating the tremor that seeps out in my voice. "You shouldn't be here, Tara."

Tara's footsteps falter and she stalls in the hallway, running obviously agitated hands through her knotted hair. She's watching me skittishly, as though she thinks she's the one who should be terrified, and not me.

"No," she says, shaking her head frantically, and pulling at her hair. "No, no, no. You don't get to ask me that. You're the one who's not supposed to be here. I told you to stay away. I told you!"

"You need to leave," I say. "Kim is on her way here, and Jimmy is going to be home any minute."

"I don't care!" she screams. "Jimmy is my boyfriend, not yours. He wants me here, not you."

"He's just my friend," I say, edging back another step, because I really don't want to risk letting her get close enough to put her hands on me again. That one shove was hard enough that I'm pretty sure I'm going to end up with a nice bruise on my shoulder. "That's it, Tara, just my friend."

"We were happy," she says. "We were going to get married and start a family, but then you came along and ruined it all. Ever since he left me for you, my life has been going to shit and it's all because you're a little whore."

"He didn't leave you for me," I say, folding my arms over my chest, attempting to hide the terror I'm feeling as I move back slowly, carefully. She continues to watch me, as though she thinks I'm seconds away from attacking her, and she's mentally calculating how she can stop me.

It puzzles me and I'm not really sure what to do. She's the one who forced her way into the apartment. She's the one who's advancing on me, but the look in her eyes, it's as though she thinks she needs to defend herself, or maybe defend Jimmy's place.

"Yes he did," she spits out. "I'm not stupid. I've been watching both of you. I know you two don't actually *work* when you're together. I've seen the way he touches you, the way he hugs you, the way he looks at you ... We're having a baby together, you bitch. Why couldn't you just find your own man!"

Crap. Jimmy is right. She's crazy, completely out of her mind nuts.

"Tara, I know you're not pregnant," I say, struggling to keep my tone even. "I know you can't have kids. This isn't the way to get him back. I can help you, though. I *will* help you. All you need to do is calm down and stop lying, okay?"

She lets out a sudden manic laugh, ringing her hands together, as her wild eyes dart around the apartment. She takes another step toward me, and I take another back.

Then, I shriek because I guess telling her that I can help her was the wrong thing to say. Or maybe it was the comment about her not being pregnant. I'm not sure.

But at the moment, it doesn't matter.

All at once, she screams and lunges at me, her hands swinging at me, her fingernails coming dangerously close to my eyes.

I scramble back into the living room, and unfortunately, in my haste to get away, I'm not paying attention to my footing, and I topple over one of the boxes in the room, landing hard on what sounds like a box filled with glass.

Tara lands on top of me, her hands frantically clawing at my face. We struggle on the floor, the glass crunching within the box under me, as more boxes topple over all around us. I can feel blood bead up on my skin as her fingernails dig into my cheeks, my neck, and my arms.

"You think I want your help?" she screeches. "I don't need your help. I don't need anyone's help. All I need is you gone. Gone and out of the picture."

I need to get away from her. I need to get to my phone, and call for help. No, scratch that. I need to get to my phone, then get to the bedroom or bathroom, lock the door, and then call for help.

I wince as her nails dig hard into the side of my jaw, scraping along my neck, and I struggle to get my arms up over my face to protect it from her attack. I buck and kick, trying to dislodge her from my center, clawing and flailing, but it seems useless. She's stronger than I am, bigger than me, and I can't get her off.

We're making quite a ruckus, I realize, as a mixture of angry and frightened tears burn my eyes. The contents of the boxes crashing onto the floor, the thumping of our limbs, our shrieks and screams. Someone is bound to hear us, and then they will come to investigate.

If I can just hold her off, stop her from doing too much damage, maybe, just maybe ...

Suddenly Tara shifts, putting all of her weight on one of her knees, planting it right in the center of my stomach, lifting herself up, and bouncing, pushing all the air from my lungs. Panic rises up fast in my throat as I struggle underneath her, my hands flailing around, searching for something—anything—I can use as a weapon.

She's reaching for something, too, I realize, as she mutters all kinds of things, about how her and Jimmy are going to get married, and how she isn't going to let some little whore like me stop her, completely unaware of my hand as I clasp onto the handle of a frying pan. I wrap my hand around the handle, good and tight, and without hesitation, I swing at her as hard as I can, hitting her firmly on the back, hard enough to dislodge her, and she falls, face first onto the floor, letting out a startled shriek.

Jumping up to my feet, my body screaming at me from the sudden movement, I scramble toward the door, the frying pan still clutched in my hand. I only make it a few steps, before I hear Tara coming after me and a second later, I feel a sharp burning sensation as something slices into my thigh, and I cry out, spinning around, blindly swinging the frying pan.

Vance

I'm sitting at a table in Heaven Here Coffee with Jase and Wes, waiting for a client to show up, when my phone rings. I pick it up off the table, glancing at the screen.

Kim.

My brow furrows. She's supposed to be at Jimmy's right now with Piper. I answer it quickly, feeling on edge as I bring the phone to my ear. "What's up?"

"Don't freak out, but you need to get over to the hospital."

"What?" My stomach coils. "Why?"

"Um ..." She lets out a shaky breath. "Tara attacked Piper."

My heart skips a beat before hammering hard in my chest as my mind starts to race, my thoughts scattered. Adrenaline washes over me, mixed with panic, and every muscle in my body constricts.

"What the fuck do you mean Tara attacked Piper?"

Silence.

Helpless anger flares through me. "Jesus Christ, Kim, tell me what the fuck is going on!"

"Piper's okay," Kim says hesitantly, her words sounding broken and strained. "She needs some stitches, but she's okay. Tara came at her with a knife, but Pipes knocked her out with a frying pan. The cops have Tara now, and Pipes is being loaded into the ambulance."

I blink.

Tara came at Piper with a knife.

Tara came at Piper with a knife.

Tara came at Piper …

My heart does something weird. There's a squeeze. There's an odd beat and skip. And my throat … my throat closes up.

My girl is hurt.

My girl.

"Fuck!" I blink again, and then I'm on my feet. "I'm on my way."

I hang up on her, shoving the phone in my pocket, and run my hands over my face roughly, when my heart squeezes and pulls and twists.

Jesus, what's wrong with me?

My eyes dart across the table when one of the guys clears his throat, and I see both Jase and Wes staring at me, eyes concerned and questioning.

Another blink. *Fuck.*

"It's Piper," I say. "I've gotta go."

I don't give them any more and I don't wait for a response, striding out of the coffee shop and sprinting for my truck.

I reach it quickly, and I don't know how, but suddenly Jase is there, blocking my path. He's standing in front of me between me and my truck, a concerned expression on his face.

"Get out of my way, Jase," I say, moving to step past him. "I have to get to the hospital."

"Just tell me what's going on first," he says, his expression serious.

"I don't know," I say. "Kim said Piper got cut when Tara came at her with a knife. Cops have Tara, and Piper's on the way to the hospital."

His brow furrows. "Wasn't she at Jimmy's? Where the fuck was he when this happened?"

"I don't know," I say again, my voice coming out as a frustrated growl. "I can't do this, Jase. I've got to go."

He hesitates, frowning at me, and then nods, stepping aside. "Go. I'll call Cruz and get the details. We'll be there soon."

I step past him and get in my truck, tires spinning as I speed away. I don't know how long it takes me to get to the hospital.

Ten minutes.

Fifteen.

It takes too goddamn long, before I see the signs for the emergency entrance. I pull in and park, which feels like it takes a fucking century to do, and then I sprint to the entrance.

It's just a cut, I tell myself. *She's okay. Kim said she's okay.*

Another century passes as I wait at the reception desk, trying to find out where my girl is. I text Kim, try to listen for her and Jimmy, scan the area for police, anything that could give me a hint of where she is, as I wait.

Nothing.

I hear nothing.

See nothing.

My stomach twists tighter.

Another few minutes pass by before I'm finally told where she is, and a nurse leads me to her room. I pause at the doorway, staring at the bed. Piper is on her back, with Kim by her side, squeezing her hand. Jimmy is in the corner, looking distressed as he stares at her, and the doctor is here, hovering over her leg. His back is to me and I can't see what he's doing, but by his arm movements, it looks like he's stitching her up now.

I swallow thickly, taking a step forward into the room.

She looks pale—paler than normal—and she grimaces with each movement of the doctor's hand.

Fuck.

I watch quietly waiting for the doctor to finish, not wanting to disturb him.

Another year passes by.

Jimmy looks up, noticing me first, and gives me a shaky chin lift. "Vance ..." His voice cracks with distress, and he wrings his hands together. "I wasn't even gone twenty minutes. I was just grabbing a pizza."

I nod. I don't know what to say to him. Logically, I know this isn't his fault.

None of it is.

But fuck if I don't want to hit him right now.

Piper leans to the side, looking around the doctor. She smiles brightly, wiping her eyes when she sees me. "I'm getting stitches again."

Her voice is just as bright as her smile, and even though there is a hint of pain beneath it, it instantly puts me at ease. "I heard. You're gonna be a pro at this in no time."

She laughs, and then cringes when the doctor tells her to hold still, and puts in another stitch.

Kim leans in, whispering something to Piper that I can't hear, before letting go of her hand, backing away. She grabs Jimmy and drags him from the room, flashing me a smile as she walks past.

Once they're gone, I move further into the room, taking up Kim's place beside Piper. She reaches her hand out to me, and it shakes slightly when I grasp onto it, squeezing it with both my hands.

The next two hours are a blur of doctors and police officers. Cruz takes her statement, and as I listen to her recount the incident, I don't know whether to be amazed with her, or furious with Jimmy.

Mostly, I'm pissed off at myself for not being there to protect her.

Cruz assures her that Tara's in lock-up. There's a chance she'll make bail and someone will post it, but he guarantees that an emergency restraining order will be put in place to protect her. Not that it matters; I'm not letting her out of my sight anytime soon.

Jase and Wes show up sometime during the statement taking and Elena is with them. I'm not entirely sure how Piper feels about the audience, but she seems to take it all in stride, smiling at everyone, thanking them for coming and telling them not to worry.

When she's finally released, I help her out to the truck. She's limping and I try to carry her, but the stubborn woman keeps shoving me away, telling me she's fine.

"You scared me, freckles," I say quietly, once I have her alone in my truck.

She looks at me, and her smile wavers. "I scared me, too. Hitting someone with a frying pan is harder than you think. I almost dropped the damn thing."

"Don't joke," I say. "This isn't funny."

"Vance …"

My mouth tightens as she tries to say something, and I hold up my hand and look her right in the eyes. "I love you. I didn't realize how much, how deep, until I got that call from Kim, but fuck, Piper, I love you."

She returns my look, her eyes holding steady, and she smiles.

That smile … It's so damn pretty.

And then she says, "I know you do."

Epilogue

About three months later ...

Piper

Vance shifts beside me and his hands slide between my thighs, pushing my legs apart.

Cracking one eye open, and then the other, I look up at him as he moves his big body between my legs. "What time is it?" I ask, my voice thick and scratchy with sleep.

He doesn't respond, merely smirks, placing a kiss on my belly, before pushing my legs open wider, and his tongue grazes over my clit. He licks and sucks, and in no time at all, I'm gasping and tugging at his hair, pleasure sweeping through me as I shudder through my orgasm.

Vance doesn't give me a second to catch my breath, before he climbs on top of me. He takes his time inside me, though, not rushing, but not hesitating either. His lips never leave my skin as he fills me over and over again.

It's beautiful.

And the sound he makes, that deep groan as he comes ...

He's beautiful.

"Best wake up ever," I mumble against his shoulder as he rolls off me.

Vance chuckles, wrapping his arms around me as I snuggle in beside him.

"Don't get too comfy," he says. "It's seven-thirty."

My brow furrows, his words not quite registering with me. "What?"

"You asked what time it is," he replies, a hint of amusement in his voice. "It's seven-thirty, which means we've got thirty minutes to shower, get dressed, and get down to the office."

Crapsicles!

We're going to be late!

We're opening up the new PRG Investigations office today, and we're supposed to be meeting the guys and Elena at the doors for eight o'clock sharp.

Jumping up in a flurry of motion, I rush to the bathroom, but I don't hear Vance move, and I stall, glancing back at him. "Get up," I say. "We can't be late for this."

"We've got lots of time." His voice is amused, and so are his eyes, but his expression is soft and sweet.

It makes my belly flutter and I like it—*a lot*.

"No we don't," I say, shaking my head, flustered as I move into the bathroom and turn on the shower, Vance's laughter following me.

God, I love that laugh.

It hasn't been all laughs and fun these last few months since my troubles ended, but it has been one hell of a ride. It's been amazing and a little scary, but mostly, perfect—even when it's not so perfect.

The trial against Tara was fairly easy to go through. I thought I would have to testify, and deal with a long and drawn out process, but she pleaded guilty and was sentenced to five years in prison for vandalism, assault with a weapon, and arson of an inhabited structure.

Vance's schedule is still crazy, and he runs off at all hours, but it doesn't matter. We never spend a night apart. My place ... His place ... One of us is always in the other's bed, but that doesn't matter, either. I don't care where we are as long as I wake up with him beside me.

Vance comes into the bathroom, pulling the shower curtain open and jumping in with me. He turns me to him, moving me back against the tiled wall, and without further warning, he kisses me, long and deep, with lots of tongue, his hands curling over my butt.

It makes me dizzy.

When his mouth pulls away, he rests his forehead against mine, his hands moving up my back, as he looks me straight in the eyes.

"Love you, Piper," he murmurs.

I smile, my heart beating wildly. He says it every day, but I swear each time I hear it, it feels like the first time. "Love you more."

He chuckles and rubs his nose against mine, before backing up a step and picking up the shampoo.

It's nearly ten minutes after eight when we reach the new office. We have to park around the corner, and make our way through the early morning rush to the building. The location is awesome, and the guys are going to be even busier than they already are when it takes off.

Jase is on the sidewalk, leaning against the door with Elena in his arms. When she sees me, she gives me a wave and smiles.

"Hey, Pipes," she says, but she barely gets the words out, over a sudden squeal of tires.

We all turn to look at the street as the sound of metal crashing together hits us, and see a shiny gray Mazda, smashed right into the back of Wes's car.

The driver's side door opens and a tall blonde-haired woman jumps out of the car. "Shit, shit, shit," she chants, making her way toward Wes as he opens his door and gets out. "I'm so ..." Her voice trails off, her footsteps stalling suddenly, and her body jerks back a step. "Shit. Of course it's you."

Wes straightens up and clears his throat, rubbing the back of his neck as he eyes her warily. "Sarah?"

His voice is strangled, and his expression, dumbfounded. I've never seen him look so ... insecure.

She walks straight up to him, hands on her hips and scowls.

"Wesley."

Vance tenses at my side, and Jase and Elena go perfectly still as we watch them stare at each other, or rather glare at each other, nose to nose, neither of them saying a word. The woman—Sarah—looks furious, which is entirely ridiculous because she's the one who rear-ended Wes, but Wes ... Well, Wes looks like he's either going to pass out or throw up.

What the heck is happening here?

"Shit," Jase mutters under his breath, exchanging a look with Vance that I can't even begin to read.

"Who's that?" Elena mock whispers, nudging Jase with her shoulder.

"That," Jase says, "is Sarah Parker, Wes's high school girlfriend. She ripped his heart out a few years back, took off with some guy in the middle of the night, not even leaving a note."

"Are you serious?" I whisper, looking from Vance to Jase.

Vance nods.

"She's gorgeous," Elena says.

Vance laughs, so does Jase, as they both move toward Wes, and Elena turns to me and says, "Huh, this should be interesting."

Acknowledgments

An enormous thank you goes to my family and friends. You all are the best support group I could ever ask for. Thank you so much for your encouragement and patience as I worked through the writing process. I love you all.

To my editor, Kathryn, I couldn't have finished this book without you. Thank you for your patience and hard work. You are an invaluable member of my team and I'm so glad to have you.

And to my husband, Jordan, thank you for believing in me.

But most of all, I would like to thank the readers, reviewers, and bloggers for your support and for sharing your love of books. You all are the reason I keep writing.

About The Author

Ashley Stoyanoff is an author of romance novels for young adult and new adult readers, including The Soul's Mark series and the Deadly Trilogy. She lives in Southern Ontario with her husband, Jordan, and two cats: Tanzy and Trinity.

In July 2012, Ashley published her first novel, The Soul's Mark: FOUND, and shortly thereafter, she was honored with The Royal Dragonfly Book Award for both young adult and newbie fiction categories.

An avid reader, Ashley enjoys anything with a bit of romance and a paranormal twist. When she's not writing or devouring her latest read, she can be found spending time with her family, watching cheesy chick flicks or buying far too many clothes.

Ashley loves hearing from her readers, so feel free to connect with her online.

www.ashleystoyanoff.com
www.facebook.com/AuthorAshleyStoyanoff
www.twitter.com/AshleyStoyanoff
www.goodreads.com/ashley_stoyanoff

54708785R00132

Made in the USA
Charleston, SC
12 April 2016